# A PLUNGE INTO SPACE

THE LAST MAN ENTERS. THE STEEL GLOBE.

*Front.*

# A PLUNGE INTO SPACE

BY

ROBERT CROMIE,

*WITH A PREFACE BY JULES VERNE.*

**Fredonia Books**
**Amsterdam, The Netherlands**

A Plunge Into Space

by
Robert Cromie

ISBN: 1-58963-600-7

Reprinted from the 1976 edition

Fredonia Books
Amsterdam, the Netherlands
http://www.fredoniabooks.com

# CONTENTS.

———◦◦———

# CONTENTS.

# A PLUNGE INTO SPACE

*A volume in the Hyperion reprint series*
# CLASSICS OF SCIENCE FICTION

## A PLUNGE INTO SPACE

Robert Cromie, a British author, achieved a considerable measure of success with a series of science fiction novels written between 1889-1902. Most of them, now all but forgotten, were on the popular "wars-of-the-future" theme, which so totally fascinated English readers between the appearance of the first of these stories (*The Battle of Dorking*, 1871) and the outbreak of World War I. Cromie's reputation, however, is based on a single book of a very different kind — probably one of the most remarkable interplanetary novels of all time: *A Plunge Into Space*. Published in 1890, it was continuously reprinted until 1910, earning the enthusiastic plaudits of Jules Verne, which are included as an introduction to the Hyperion edition. Much of the scientific material is unusually prophetic, but what is extraordinary is the vivid drama developed as a result of the harsh necessities of space as opposed to human needs. (This theme was used in a modern science fiction classic, *The Cold Equations*, by Tom Godwin, published in 1954). A group of scientific adventurers builds a space ship for the purpose of exploring Mars. The motor device is a shield that protects against earth's gravity while being attracted to Mars. (This probably inspired a similar device in H.G. Wells' *The First Men on the Moon*, 1901). On the return trip they discover a stowaway — a Martian girl. The life-support systems of the ship cannot accomodate an extra passenger, and each crew member has some essential skill for bringing the ship safely to earth. The drama builds with enormous tension to a fateful climax as the girl becomes the key to life — or death — for the space voyagers.

TO

## JULES VERNE,

To whom I am indebted for many delightful
and marvellous excursions—notably, a voyage
from the earth to the moon, a trip twenty
thousand leagues under the sea and a journey
round the world in eighty days—and who,
in return, has now courteously consented to
accompany me to the planet Mars, at the
rate of fifty thousand miles a minute,

*I DEDICATE THIS BOOK.*

**ROBERT CROMIE.**

BELFAST,
    *February 1891.*

# A PLUNGE INTO SPACE

# A PLUNGE INTO SPACE.

## CHAPTER I.

### PROLOGUE.

"It moves at last! MacGregor, *it moves!*"

"Why not? Let it move again, by all means.",

After a few moments' silence MacGregor said in the same careless voice, which contrasted strongly with the quivering breathless accents of the first speaker:

"Come out of that wizard's cave, Barnett, and be social. Consider that it is more than three years since I have seen your profoundly scientific face. Let that thing, whatever it is, move as much as it likes, and let me have a look at you."

From an inner room opening off that in which Mac-Gregor sat, the excited voice came nervously:

"Hush, for mercy's sake; just one minute more!" Then, at the sound of MacGregor's footsteps crossing the room, there was almost a scream : "Don't come near me, MacGregor. Don't stir for your life. Remain where you are at your peril."

"I am not at all likely to visit you, I assure you," Alexander MacGregor muttered. "I don't want to blow up half the square by treading on the spring of one of your infernal machines, or by brushing my head inadvertently against some of your wires, knobs, buttons, or batteries—Beard a lion in his den! What's a lion's den to a scientist's laboratory!"

With this reflection Mr. MacGregor settled himself comfortably on a low couch by a bright fire in the cosy little room, lit his pipe, and waited for his eccentric host to appear. It was pleasant enough to lie there and smoke, and listen lazily to the faint click—click—hiss— and anon a tiny explosion which sounded incessantly in the inner room, and watch with drowsy eyes the curious flashes of blue, red, or white light which sparkled through the curtained doorway. The reclining guest was neither surprised nor hurt at the cool reception he had received. In fact, he was rather amused. It was so characteristic of Barnett.

"What a strange creature he is!" came dreamily through the smoke wreaths. " Here am I, just arrived in London from Tibet, where I have been exploring for three years, and have been reported as dead at least a dozen times. I enter the house of my oldest friend. He tells me not to stir for my life; not to come near him at my peril! Hospitable, certainly! But it's all right; he is inventing something; he will have a lucid interval presently. Meantime, I am very comfortable."

The explorer had almost dropped asleep, when a stifled exclamation, more like a sob than a sentence, in the laboratory aroused him. As he listened to the deep breathing of his friend, who was now oblivious of everything but his experiment, MacGregor said half sadly to himself:

"Poor Barnett; what a splendid fellow he was at Cambridge long ago! That den of his will be his death!"

The "den," indeed, was an excellent specimen of those factories incidental to civilisation, where you put in raw material, in the shape of human beings, at one end, and turn out an equal number of perfect machines at the other—excepting, of course, those brittle souls which go to smash in the process.

Henry Barnett had spent the best years of his life in this room. He had disappeared into it, some twenty years before, a straight, muscular young man, with a rather large head. He now emerged from it to greet MacGregor, a stooped and wasted middle-aged man, with a head out of all proportion to his shrivelled frame.

"Whatever is the matter with you, Barnett?" MacGregor asked anxiously.

The singular host did not shake hands with his guest, nor extend to him the slightest form of welcome. He trembled visibly, and his breath came in broken gasps as he said, without a word of explanation:

"MacGregor, you have arrived at an opportune moment."

"Humph! It looks like it. I have been here an hour."

"Yes, MacGregor," Henry Barnett went on, without noticing the interruption; "I am grateful for your visit this evening of all others."

"Don't mention it, Barnett. Your instinct of hospitality is too keen," the explorer remarked coolly, as he refilled his pipe.

Barnett went to a sideboard, poured out a glass of water, and drank it off. Then he mopped his forehead with his handkerchief and wiped his moist and trembling hands.

"He's out of his mind, as sure as fate. I must carry him off to the seaside for a month," MacGregor reflected.

The scientist recrossed the room, and said impressively:

"Alexander MacGregor, come with me into my workshop."

This new trick of ceremoniously addressing the companion of half a lifetime confirmed MacGregor's suspicions.

"I—I—would rather not, Barnett. I am not much of a coward, but I—I don't like those confounded wires and springs and things. I'll be certain to blow up some of your electric devilries."

"No, no, there is no danger. Come with me."

"Ahem!—Well, I suppose I must."

The two men entered the inner room together. To the casual observer their movements would have suggested burglary. Barnett walked unsteadily; his failing constitution had just received a severe shock. His limbs hardly supported him. And MacGregor, great brown-bearded, stern-eyed, leather-visaged traveller as he was—hero of a hundred fights with man and beast and natural forces, bears in the Rockies, blacks in the Congo, simooms in Arabia, and cyclones in the China seas—he wriggled along in a ridiculous tiptoe fashion.

The laboratory was not very terrifying in appearance. It was a dusty little chamber. "Cleaning up" was unknown to it. The voice of the painter had not been heard in it for many a day, or year. Even the evidence of the more humble plasterer's handicraft was sadly lacking. But what it wanted in decoration it made up for in the quaintness of its furniture. Here were tiers of little moth-eaten drawers. There lay great coils of wire. Wide-mouthed bottles, glass tubes of various shapes, air-pumps, chemical balances, crucibles, and spirit lamps were strewn about in great confusion. Electric machines of novel design were ranged beside the types familiar to every student. Fragments of a curious grey substance were lying amid pieces of metallic leaf and little balls of elder-pith and downy feathers. The room was a medley of ordinary and extraordinary devices.

"Read that," Barnett said, thrusting a paper covered with figures, letters, signs, and tokens, into MacGregor's hand.

"It is very interesting—very interesting indeed," MacGregor remarked with a wise look. The paper was as unintelligible to him as Egyptian hieroglyphics. But poor Barnett's mind was evidently unhinged; it was necessary to be gentle with him.

"What do you think of it?" Barnett asked eagerly.

"Think of it!" MacGregor exclaimed, driven into a corner. "Oh, as to that, I dare say it is all right." Then blankly, as he turned the paper upside down, looked at it on this side and on that: "What is it all about?"

Barnett snatched the paper back impatiently.

"Do you see that ball?" he asked, with a shade of contempt in his voice which nettled MacGregor, in spite of his previous compassion. Whereupon the explorer declared, with some asperity, that his intelligence was equal to the moderate task appointed.

The ball, a tiny sphere, was lying in a tube of glass. This tube stood in an upright position on a plate of that strange grey material; whether it was vegetable or mineral, MacGregor could not decide.

" Watch it now ! "

Barnett laid the end of a thin wire on the grey substance.  The ball within the tube flew to its upper end and remained there, suspended, as it were, by a magnet.

The scientist literally shook in his shoes with excitement.  The explorer politely pretended to admire the experiment, but privately thought it uninteresting.  " Ha ! Very pretty ! " he remarked by way of compliment.

" Pretty, MacGregor !   Think what you are saying ! "

" Well, I mean that it is——"

Barnett interrupted with a gesture.

" Listen to me," he said in a voice that strengthened as he went on, while his bent frame straightened out, and his pale, deep-lined face flushed red.   " In this room I have worked for twenty years."

" More fool ! " MacGregor muttered.

" Twenty years devoted, consecrated to a glorious work ! You, my friend MacGregor, like all my neighbours, have, I doubt not, pitied me as a poor enthusiast—a mere theorist, whose dreary years dragged slowly by in a useless sequence of drivelling dreams."

MacGregor made a deprecating gesture.

" You have pitied me because I rotted within these four walls while you climbed the snowy mountain peak, or sailed the heaving seas.  You have wondered, I am sure, how slowly passed my lonely days in such a dismal

den. Bah! My years were as days, and my days but
moments."

MacGregor became attentive. There may have been
some strong purpose in this weak-minded dreamer after
all. He listened intently as Barnett, carried away by his
own thoughts, declaimed with unconscious dramatic force:

"You, MacGregor, have done good service to your
country and, indeed, to your race. You have tracked
many a mighty river to its hitherto unknown source;
you have plunged into gloomy forests, impenetrable until
your restless feet had gauged their depths; and you
have your reward. I ask, do you now regret the lonely
years spent in Africa, Asia, on the Pacific, Arctic and
Antarctic seas?"

"No," said MacGregor emphatically and with increasing interest. Barnett might be mad, but even a madman
must be unconscionably silly to render his praise of one's
own hobby unwelcome.

"Are you better satisfied to stand here, the greatest
explorer the world has known (MacGregor shook his
head negatively, but not displeased), or, for the saving of
a few streaks of grey in your hair and lines on your face,
would you prefer to have passed your life in the sodden
atmosphere of ignoble ease?"

"No!" MacGregor shouted fiercely.

"Then, do you pity me now when I tell you that I
have discovered——"

He sprang to the window, and tore the curtains aside. The night was clear. A white hoar-frost lay on the patch of trampled grass which the genteel suburban residents called a park. The sky glistened with starry brilliance.

"Look, MacGregor!"

Both men gazed up at that vast sidereal host of heaven, whose fearful immensity appals a finite mind. Barnett lowered his voice to a solemn cadence, and continued:

"Do you pity me now when I tell you that after twenty paltry years of work, I have discovered the origin and essence of that law which, before me, never man did aught but name, or, at best, did but chronicle its known effects—the law which makes that universe of worlds a grand well-ordered army instead of a helpless mob of mutually destroying forces; when I tell you that within this ragged room, there stands a man who—grant him but ten years of human life—could sway a star in its course, could hurl a planet from its path? Man, I have discovered the mightiest secret of creation!"

He stopped abruptly, his deep emotion had overcome his power of speech. He clasped and unclasped his hands nervously. His face worked convulsively. The man was overwhelmed by the majesty of his own discovery, now that the end—notwithstanding it had long been foreseen—was come.

"Barnett, Barnett, are you really mad?"

"Yes, mad enough, for I hold in my brain that which a human soul may hardly keep and hope to live."

"To drop this rhodomontade, Barnett, what the devil is it you have discovered? You said my visit was opportune—I assume you mean to tell me."

"I do."

"Then out with it in plain English. In what have your experiments culminated?"

"I have discovered the origin——"

He bent lower, and whispered hoarsely:

"Of—*force*!"

"Come out, Barnett. This room is suffocating," MacGregor exclaimed feverishly.

They sat down in the adjoining room. Neither spoke for some time. In a sense, the silence was oppressive, but each man was too busy with his own thoughts to break it. The fire burned low; neither replenished it. A gas jet flamed and fumed. Neither attended to it. And yet both felt the room grow cold, and both were wearied by the persistent whistle of the gas jet. MacGregor spoke at last.

"Will you describe to me exactly, Barnett, how you expect to use this great discovery?"

"I am unable as yet to collect my thoughts sufficiently to be intelligible. I am still dazed, stupefied. Remember that, after twenty years of work, the actual climax of the discovery is hardly an hour old."

"Granted; but at least you can name some main tendency of the inventions which you will found on this knowledge."

"Yes, I could name one."

"And that is——"

"The experiment with the glass tube shows that the law of gravitation may be diverted, directed, or destroyed. I can elaborate and perfect the mechanism necessary for the development of this discovery. The results must be such as would at present appear inconceivable."

MacGregor leaped to his feet. It was his turn now.

"Listen to me, Henry Barnett," he said, unconsciously imitating the other man's stilted style and melodramatic tones. "You *shall* develop that mechanism." Here he brought down his great brown fist with a bang on the table near which Barnett sat. This table was not a costly piece of furniture, and that portion of it which met the impact of MacGregor's fist was a movable leaf, not very strongly supported. The moth-eaten woodwork gave way and fell on the scholar's slippered feet!

"Oh bother it! I did not know it was so flimsy. I beg your pardon a thousand times, Barnett."

But the scholar would not be comforted—and he who could hurl a planet from its path confessed to corns.

It was impossible, MacGregor felt, to renew the heroic style. So he described in simple but vivid language, the scheme which had flashed into his active brain, whereby the grand discovery might be grandly used. Several hours passed in an eager discussion, and it was very late when the men thought of sleep. Before retiring to their rooms, they seized each other's hands in a long and meaning clasp, and each man pledged himself to devote his life to the furtherance of the great scheme, to record the history of which this book has been written. Then, after some trivial remarks on current topics, they said " Good-night," in the most conventional accents, and separated.

Thus simply ended the prologue to the strangest drama ever enacted by mortal man.

# CHAPTER II.

### A FOREST FOUNDRY.

WITHIN an Alaskan forest, Henry Barnett and Alexander MacGregor are seated on a pine trunk, conversing with languid interest. Their eyes turn frequently towards a pass in the lofty mountains by which their sheltered valley is surrounded on all sides. They are expecting visitors.

It is the month of June. The mountains are still snow-capped, but in the valley the air is very warm; roses are budding on the slope which faces due south. A year ago this valley had rarely borne a human footmark —once in a season, perhaps, a half-starved Indian may have crossed it. Now hundreds of men live in it. It is situated in the richest mineral region of Alaska. The mountain ranges around it contain the head waters of three of the Territory's most important rivers—the Copper, the White, and the Tananá.

MacGregor has not changed one iota since that night when he visited his friend in a commonplace London suburb, and learned a fateful secret. His tanned face

and hands could not have well become browner or more
weather-beaten.   His keen grey eyes could hardly have
sparkled with a brighter light than a lifetime of adventure had long since burned into them; his frame could
not have grown more stalwart, nor could his physical
courage have been intensified.

With Barnett it is different.   His figure is more erect,
his cheek less pale, his eyes brighter, and his whole
bearing more robust than of old, when he spent all his
days and half his nights in that little room, fittingly
described by MacGregor as a "wizard's cave."   For nearly
twelve months he has hardly opened a book, and instead
he has wielded sledge and hammer.   He has roamed the
gorges of the Alaskan mountains while puzzling out some
knotty point in silence, instead of stewing in a musty
room with an eight-foot ceiling.   Above all, there is
stamped upon his features the consciousness of success.

The fitful conversation which the two men were keeping up gradually ceased, until absolute silence reigned—
absolute silence only in so far as the speakers themselves
were concerned, for from the woods behind there came
noise enough for a shipyard.   The din, which was at
times almost deafening, did not seem to disturb either of
the men.   In fact they were not aware of it.   They had
grown accustomed to it.

" See, here they come ! "   MacGregor suddenly exclaimed, in great joy, pointing at the same time to

a cleft in the mountain, through which a rough track ran.

In numbers they were a strong party, but their pace was slow, and every horse and every horseman showed symptoms of extreme fatigue. Five gentlemen rode together in front. In the rear struggled a band of tired men on tired animals, driving, flogging, cursing on, a heavily loaded mule train.

"Bravo, Sir George! We shall dine to-night, Barnett," the brawny Scotchman said, with unction. "Trust Sterling to bring his larder—ay, and his cellar— with him. I would know those cases anywhere. Come, let us ride down and meet them. The least we can do is to bid them welcome to our Arcadian forest. Ugh! hear that!" A scream more demoniacal than usual had flung its nerve-splitting crash over the pine tops.

"You had better go, MacGregor, and make my excuses. You know I do not ride comfortably."

"Very well. I shall not be long away."

In a few moments MacGregor was mounted and cantering smartly down the slope to meet the coming cavalcade.

Barnett remained seated on the pine trunk. For some time his face had an anxious expression, and his brows were knit. Once or twice he muttered aloud, "How will it end; how will it all end?" Presently the look of care passed away, and he was just settled comfortably to some mental feat of strength—approximating the length of line required to sound the stellar depths, or some such simple conundrum—when MacGregor's loud voice brought him back with a jerk to terrestrial trivialities.

"Now then, gentlemen, come this way, and I shall present you to the greatest man living, or who has ever yet lived. Afterwards you shall have your tubs, and we shall dine. Delicious word! So far we have only fed. Tonight we shall dine, thanks to your admirable commissariat, Sterling."

The men dismounted, and assembled in a group around Barnett, who had risen to meet them. By this time the sky was gloaming with the failing light of the setting sun. The pine trees threw gigantic shadows over the withered and down-trodden prairie grass. From behind the line of trees, to the astonishment of the new-comers, came that strange rumble and roar, and sounds as of mighty hammers crashing. Long streamers of leaping flame shot up blood-red against the sombre clouds, and played havoc with the stillness of the primeval forest. There was an eerie air of mystery about that mountain glen which every man acknowledged, save one—MacGregor. He was in boisterously good spirits.

"Gentlemen," he said, facetiously, "you will please answer to your names."

A look of amused consent flitted over the faces of the tired travellers.

" Mr. Barnett, this is Sir George Sterling," waving his hand towards a powerful man of full habit, dark whiskers, and a business-like air. " A financier in search of a new speculation. We shall be able to provide that. Don't you think so, my colleague ? "

Barnett smiled gravely, and murmured some words of welcome as he shook hands with the capitalist. The man of money having been presented, MacGregor was less precise in his ceremonial with the other persons of the baser sort. He merely ran over their names, and indicated their personality with a nod, thus :

"Mr. Walter Durand"—a tall, handsome, dark-haired, dark-eyed man—" a literary man in search of a new plot."

" Mr. Victor Graves "—a fair-haired, bearded man, with a pipe—" an artist in search of a new subject."

" Mr. Charles Blake "—a mirthful-looking Irishman— "a politician in search of a post."

" And Mr. Frederick Gordon "—a wiry, fleshless man, with a determined cast of features—" a special correspondent in search of copy."

Barnett exchanged a courteous bow with each as his name was mentioned, and the introductions were over. MacGregor then led the way along a pathway through the trees. In a few minutes they reached a wide clearing, and found a long, low, wooden house, surrounded by a neatly kept grass plot. Here they were to live for some pleasant, idle weeks.

When the travellers had exchanged their wayworn clothes for fresh garments, they assembled in the large common room, or dining-hall. Dinner was served with something of the pomp and circumstance naturally attending that important ceremony. It was a plentiful meal, if wanting in the more delicate details which turn a mere animal necessity into an important social function. The forest and the river, a tributary of the Copper, had been requisitioned for their very best. Salmon fresh run, river trout, rabbits, shoulder of *tcbáy*, joint of caribou, moose nose, blue grouse, wild duck, and such toothsome viands, added to the vast array of cunningly preserved meats, and drinks, and relishes furnished by the baronet's huge packages, made no poor show upon the festive board. To men who had been in the saddle for a week in the lively air of the Alaskan hills, it was a royal feast.

And it must not be forgotten that from the depths of Sir George's packages had also proceeded divers bottles, square in shape, and adorned with much sealing-wax about the corks, the contents of which not even a mule trot could spoil. These seals were quickly broken, and the bottles square passed gaily round.

Barnett sat silent and thoughtful, but MacGregor kept the company alternately thrilled and amused by well-told stories of his wild, rambling life. Under his genial influence, assisted possibly by the well-matured spirit in those great bottles, the men who had spent the previous week in vicious grumbling and almost openly avowed distaste for each other's society, began to wonder at their own stupidity. When had they enjoyed such a feast, or met such pleasant company? Why, every man was a prince of good fellows—now that they knew themselves aright!

When dinner was over, and cigars lighted, the company divided into two parties. One consisted of the baronet, MacGregor and Barnett. They, it was evident, had matters of business to discuss; and if one might judge from the long rows of figures, every row having on its left margin that mighty symbol £, their business was finance.

The other party fast increased and multiplied in their own and their companions' esteem. An interchange of confidences, which had been rigorously withheld for many weary days was now inevitable.

" I say, Durand," the artist broke out; " suppose you tell us what your plans are—what brought you here, in point of fact."

" You heard MacGregor," Durand answered, laughing. " A new plot."

" Rubbish! You don't expect a new plot in this primeval region. Blake might as well look here for his post."

" What, then, about your new subject ? "

" And what about my ' copy ' ? " Gordon put in.

"Suppose we all give our experiences," Blake suggested. "Perhaps in that way we may find out what brought us all here. You begin Durand."

"Well, then," Durand said, "I got a letter from Mac-Gregor consisting of about four lines, telling me that if I wanted to make the sensational writers green with envy, I must come out by the S.S. Arizona, which sailed, as you know, on the 15th of last month. Of course he gave me particulars as to where the guides would meet us when the little steamer from Vancouver Island, which he had chartered, set us ashore. I knew the man so well that I never doubted but he had his eye on some new ground in China, or Central Asia, or some other outlandish place. I had nothing else to do. The beaten track of the British novelist is inconveniently crowded at present, so here I am."

"I received a similar note," Gordon said. "Mac-Gregor told me that if I wanted to lay the names of all the 'specials' who have gone before me in the dust, I should book my passage in the Arizona. I did feel that I should like to carry out this suggestion, and so here I am."

Graves, the artist, had a similar experience. In his case, he was to put the entire school of artistic masters, old and young, in the shade, and as he found that to hit off his ambition pretty closely, he came likewise.

"Faith," said Blake, "he promised me a post, and, as

things go nowadays, I never dreamed of asking what it was."

"Nor whether you were qualified to fill it?" Durand asked drily.

"Qualified! My dear fellow, I am qualified for anything;" hastily, "I mean any post. I am a politician."

"If we did not know MacGregor so well," Gordon said again, "don't you think we might all feel rather silly now that we are here and have found—a wooden house, or hut, and a primeval forest enlivened only by that infernal din of hammering somewhere near."

"Don't be afraid of losing your time. MacGregor is sure to keep his word," Durand said positively. "I venture to say he will surprise us all before long."

He certainly did surprise them, and that too before ten minutes had elapsed. His voice broke in upon their conversation.

"Now gentlemen, the night air is cold, although the days at this season are very warm here. Light fresh cigars, put on your heavy cloaks, and we shall show you our works."

"Your what?"

"Our works."

"What sort of works, in the name of wonder?"

"Smelting works, foundries, coal mines, iron mines, steam hammers, furnaces, winches, cranes, tool shops and all the rest. Come along."

MacGregor walked out followed by Barnett and Sir George Sterling. For some moments the other men looked at each other in amazement. Then they followed their hosts.

A short avenue ran through a dense wood which clothed one of the low sloping hills near the hut. This should have been as dark as midnight. To the wonder of the bewildered strangers it was as bright as noon. Two rows of powerful electric lights lined the pathway, one on either side, and between them the party walked. What might be called the solid men of the company—that is, the scientist, the explorer, and the capitalist—walked in front. The others—who, take them as you will, but look on and talk about, write about, paint about, or report about what men of action achieve—walked, as in duty bound, behind. As might be expected, each party criticised the other.

" What do you fellows think of our scientific friend ? " Durand asked.

" He seems a nice sort of man, if he were not so supernaturally calm and quiet. Still, there is something out of the common about him," Gordon replied. " I wonder where MacGregor picked him up, and what he means to do with him. That introduction was pretty strong—' the greatest man who ever lived '—and so forth ! "

" Oh, he is MacGregor's trump card in this business,

whatever it is," Blake declared. "Did any of you hear how he treated the mighty traveller on his return from that Central Asian journey of his which made such a stir?"

"No."

"Well, it is said that MacGregor, who had just arrived from Mongolia, went straight to Barnett's house on the very day he landed. The man of science was in his laboratory, working out whether the moon is really made of green cheese or choice Cheshire. So his visitor had to wait half a day before he would speak to him."

"They are an odd pair, certainly."

"And the baronet?"

"He is a fortunate man."

"How?"

"He has brains; that is excellent—he has money; that is magnificent."

In front, MacGregor asked Sir George:

"Don't you think these are a good set of men?"

"Good!" exclaimed the baronet in dismay. "Good! There is not a man in the lot good for fifty pounds. I sincerely trust, MacGregor, that you have not obliged any of them."

"Oh, I don't mean good in the financial sense," MacGregor answered testily. "And I have 'obliged' some of them. Is it very wrong to oblige a man simply because he stands in need of one's assistance?"

"Wrong, MacGregor!   Pooh, pooh!   It's a thousand times worse."

"Eh ?"

"It's bad business," Sir George said decisively.

By this time both parties had rounded an abrupt angle caused by a tremendous rock which blocked the path.

The noise in front had been increasing as they advanced.  It now became deafening.  A few more steps and all stood still, amazed.

The pathway ended in a wooden balcony built high over a gorge which swept away from the steep cliff on which the woodwork had been erected.  A pandemonium was below.  Long lines of sheds, lit every one with the incandescent glare of electric light, stretched down the hollow.  Terrible furnaces seethed and raged.  Great streams of molten metal gurgled and sparkled and shot up showers of hissing spangles as it filled huge ladles, or was poured into cunningly constructed moulds : here the starlike flame of blue-white blazing brass ; there the ruddier tint of iron.  Swarthy smiths were at work hammering and fashioning strange devices, some familiar, some fantastic, some fiendish.  Sooty demons poked and probed, and fetched and carried undismayed great tanks of liquid fire.  Mighty cranes were swaying to and fro. Giant hammers crashed and smote on yielding bars of red hot steel.  And fierce fanged saws, with demoniac shriek, tore riotously through the massive metal plates. Resistless planes crushed silently backwards and forwards. A thousand wheels whirled wildly. And above all that carnival of smoke and flame and blazing steel a curious relic of the desecrated forest floated faintly— the pungent perfume of the pines.

As the men stood there gazing on the strange scene, the seriousness of the still unknown mission was brought home to all, and every man asked himself what was this to which he had consented.

No late sitting was made that night. A week on horseback through a wild country was a sufficient guarantee against such unwisdom. As a move was being made for the various bunks—they could hardly be called bedrooms—MacGregor was seen to wrap himself in a heavy fur-cloak and cap, which only exposed two keen eyes, the tip of a bronzed nose, and the glowing end of a cigar.

" Good night, everybody," he said cheerily, as he opened the main door.

" Where are you off to now, MacGregor ? "

" To make my rounds," he answered briefly, and passed out.

# CHAPTER III.

## THE INDIAN'S FATE.

AFTER breakfast next morning, MacGregor delivered an advice to the younger men.

"We shall have nothing for any of you fellows to do for some weeks yet. An accident—one of many, I am sorry to say—in a very important casting has delayed our enterprise. Hunt, fish, shoot. You will find sport of all sorts within easy distance. Here are rods and guns. We can also lend you mounts until your own horses are recovered."

So the young men betook themselves to the forest and the river-side; shot caribou, moose, wild sheep, or bear; killed abnormal salmon that were stupendous in fact as well as in reminiscence; and, for a time, found their occupations very agreeable. Of course they wondered much, over their pipes of an evening, what the meaning of all the smelting, and casting, and steam-hammering hard by could be. But, being in their several ways somewhat of a philosophic turn, they took the life as they found it, and left their senior , headed by that forceful

chief, MacGregor, to work out their own mysterious pro-
jects unquestioned.    This pleasant, holiday life was interrupted by a tragic incident.

"I can't make out that man, Barnett," Blake said one
evening.    "He is the strangest type I ever met, so pre-
occupied and yet so polite; so grave and yet so tolerant
of all our little levities.    He disappears in the morning a
model of cleanliness; he returns in the evening as sooty
as a chimney-sweep.    Before he leaves, he is too absent-
minded to talk; when he gets back, he seems too tired."

"I don't believe he knows our names yet," Gordon
remarked.    "He always addresses whoever sits next to
him as ' Mr. ——.' "

Durand and Graves both declared he was charming.
The first had already worked him into a three-volume
novel, with about the usual want of novelty, which he had
commenced, and the second hoped one day to paint him
as the prisoner of Chillon, or other equally original figure.
Gordon had made no copy of him so far.    He had not
yet *done* anything unusual.

"Then as to MacGregor," Blake continued, "is he
possessed of a devil ? "

"He is certainly possessed of a devilish useful man
when he has got hold of Sir George Sterling," Gordon
answered.    "That man must be worth at least—" he
turned over the leaves of his note-book, but was unable
to find the entry.

"Now then, for dinner!" The cheery voice of Mac-Gregor himself broke in. Barnett and the baronet, who were seated in a distant corner, arose and pat away regretfully, certain sheets they had been poring over. The figures which covered Barnett's sheets must have had many different values, to judge from those curious little marks, accents, and qualifying sub-figures so dear to the mathematician, by which they were adorned, enhanced, or modified. The figures on the baronet's sheets were nearly as multitudinous, but of signs or qualifications there was only one—that before mentioned-symbol which indicates pounds sterling.

The feast, in the main, was furnished by the spoil of the sportsmen. Additional features had been supplied by a liberal contribution from Sir George's packages, which were holding out well. Only a distant hum could be heard from the works, once the outer door of the hut was closed. It was the time of day most enjoyed by the tired hunters of the forest, and also by the weary man of science, notwithstanding his grave silence. Indeed, it is a time of day enjoyed by many who have never hunted in a forest, nor fatigued their brains with science. And yet, the indomitable MacGregor waxed duller when he should have naturally increased in brightness.

"I am afraid, Sterling, your appearance here so soon was a mistake," he said, with unusual solemnity. "It would have been better if you had kept out of the way until we were quite ready. You could have sent us the weekly remittances for wages as at first."

" A mistake ! How so ? "

" I don't like the look of some of these rascally half-breeds. A trusty man of mine tells me that they suspect some of your baggage to consist of good gold coin."

" What if they do ? "

" They would think very little of cutting all our throats for the cash, if we were not so well armed."

" Then we have nothing to fear."

" Not from them, perhaps, but the story has got about, and those San Francisco men that we never could get to do anything, are loafing about making speeches on your tremendous wealth, their hard work, poor pay, and so on. A strike would not suit us, now that we are on the eve of success."

The sporting discussion, which usually went on at the table, by this time had lost interest for the party, and every one listened as Sir George said, somewhat sharply :

" I wish you had let me know how far behind you were, and I should have remained another month in Columbia."

" It was those disastrous mistakes in the great casting that delayed us. The whole thing had to be commenced *de novo* after every failure."

" They were not mistakes," Barnett said quietly. " They were accidents, due to the inexperience of the men."

"Well, I know you were not to blame, Barnett, but it amounts to the same thing. In any case, there is more unpleasant news."

"More!"

"Yes, more. The half-breeds are tampering with a party of Blackfeet Indians who strayed up here after Riel's rebellion. I had better tell you at once—they mean to attack the camp to-night."

MacGregor spoke in the coolest voice, but every man except himself and Barnett leaped to his feet.

"Attack the camp!"

"So I said."

"And you sit there——"

"Don't trouble yourselves, gentlemen. Our good friend here" (nodding towards Barnett) "has arranged for them."

The crack of a rifle-shot rang out close to the hut, and in the distance a faint whoop could be heard.

The men again sprang up, but MacGregor said peremptorily, "Don't move; just keep out of the line of the window when I open the iron shutter."

Barnett arose and touched a button in the wall. The light went out, and MacGregor drew aside the metal shutter. Outside all was in darkness. Another snap of a rifle, evidently only a signal, and Barnett pressed another spring.

For fully half a mile on every side the woods flashed into brilliant light. Here, there, from tree to tree, the glare of electric lamps burst forth, and with their appearance a yell of fear went up from fifty crouching Indian braves. The attack was over before it had commenced. The children of the forest thought the day of Judgment was at hand, and with cries of terror they prostrated themselves before the wizard to whom they ascribed its advent.

MacGregor, surrounded by his friends, all well armed, went out and accepted their submission.

It was none too soon, for, hurrying from the works at the sound of the first rifle-shot, the discontented half-breeds came on at a run. Armed with hammers, sledges, bars of iron, and the like, they rushed up, anxious to join in the loot. These in turn were followed by the better-class smiths and artificers, who were careless how the fight went, and were interested only to side with the victors. The situation was still critical, for although the party in front of the hut were well supplied with quick-firing rifles and revolvers, the odds against them in numbers were terribly great. Fortunately the sight of the Indian warriors on their knees knocked the fighting spirit out of the half-breeds. They slowed down in their advance, halted and huddled up foolishly, then began to give ground and scramble back.

But the Indian chief knew the secret of the electric light, or rather he knew by repute the grave white man whose fame had already travelled far as a mighty conjurer. He cursed his own people very sincerely for their timidity, and when the sullen smiths were retiring, and his own pardoned braves were slinking off, cowed and humiliated, he stole unperceived behind the Englishmen.   Feeling sure that he had only to kill the white medicine-man to secure a general victory, he crept up silently, snake-like, to within a couple of yards of his conqueror.   In the glare of the electric light, two eyeballs gleamed savagely ; a knife flashed whitely as it plunged down with a terrible swoop, and Barnett fell forward on the grass.

Had it not been for MacGregor's quick hand and iron grip, the forest foundry would have been silent next day. As. it was, the scientist had got an ugly wound.   The Indian was down in a second with MacGregor's knee on his chest, and his giant fingers on his throat.   The sulky half-breeds began to straggle back again towards the hut, muttering sullenly.   The cowed Indians shook off something of their terror, and grouped themselves in an angry, menacing crowd.   The stolid smiths looked on.   Thus nearly two hundred savage cut-throats were seething round the hut ready at a word, had any dared to give it, to spring upon their quarry.   Two of the weaker side were already *hors de combat*, one wounded badly, one holding down his enemy.   In front of these two, the five other men lined out silently, rifle in hand, cartridge pouches open—ready.

" Good men and true," MacGregor said hoarsely. "But

one of you cover this hound with your rifle until I see to Barnett. He is bleeding terribly. Let the rest stand ready to commence firing the moment those curs advance an inch."

The nearest of the five riflemen stepped back and placed the muzzle of his weapon to the Indian's head. The others kept their ground.

Barnett's stab was staunched roughly. While tying it up, MacGregor was heard to press the wounded man for exact instructions on some point or plan.

"Try every other way first, MacGregor," Barnett urged in a weak voice. "It is too terrible."

"Nonsense! What is one man's life to a hundred. Don't you see that a fight to the death is certain unless we can disperse them? Do you think they will stand there looking at us harmlessly all night?"

"Then listen. Stoop down, MacGregor, for I am very weak and it pains me to speak."

MacGregor stooped down and listened carefully, saying as he arose: "Set your mind at rest, Barnett, I tell you it is necessary." Then in the hard masterful voice he sometimes used: "I have decided that it shall be done."

Meanwhile the two sides were standing ready—one terrible in numbers, the other in weapons—each waiting for the other to begin.

"Gentlemen," MacGregor said, coming forward to the line of riflemen, and speaking very low; "this Indian must die, or we. They will attack us in five minutes if they are not dispersed. Our lives hang by a hair. I put it to your votes, and choose quickly. I myself say that the man has justly forfeited his life. What say you?"

"We say the same," solemnly answered all.

"The rest is then simple," MacGregor said, and immediately ran to where the Indian lay, covered by Gordon's rifle. Putting the muzzle of his revolver to the chieftain's head, he ordered him to march. Together, the two passed out on the open square in front of the hut.

"Stand there," MacGregor said fiercely, and the Indian felt his moccasined feet slip on some smooth substance. He obeyed sullenly.

Then MacGregor roared in his great voice: "Now then, gather round—you here—you there," and he assigned stations to the Indians, the half-breeds, and the smiths. The crowds sulkily took up their places as directed, but an ominous growl was gathering strength amongst them.

MacGregor then called out by name the man whom he had known to be stirring up the half-breeds. The fellow hesitated, but seeing the apparent fairness of the proposed meeting of generals half-way between each army, he finally yielded, and slouched over to where the captive and his gaoler stood in the centre of the open space. In the light of the powerful lamps the scene was as clear as day. The lowering faces of the encircling mob, and the five high-strung but firm white faces of the men who waited for the attack were almost ghastly in its glare.

" Better ground your arms, gentlemen. You will not need them, I think," MacGregor said, as he advanced to meet the leader of the revolt. When a yard or two only separated them, he said suddenly :

" Here, you fellow, hand that to your friend, or I will shoot you where you stand."

The sooty ruffian was taken by surprise. He mechanically accepted a heavy plug of bright metal which Mac-Gregor handed to him, and went over to where the Indian stood, with an air of reckless bravado.

Henry Barnett, weak as he was, raised himself from the ground, and turned his back on the scene. MacGregor sternly faced it out.

The Indian took the metal bar with the same sullen indifference he had shown in everything since his capture. His hand closed on the bar and instantaneously his frame drew up rigid. For a second or two he stood stiff and deathlike, and no man spoke. Then before the eyes of the horror-stricken crowd, the man's body sank down into a shapeless mass of pulp.

MacGregor tapped the half-breed on the shoulder, pointed significantly to the hideous heap, and said : " Be-gone, and take your people with you." To a foreman smith who had secretly wished to side with the owners — only their party was so inconveniently small—he said :

" Bring a couple of men and bury that mess. It is quite harmless now. The connection is off."

No second order was necessary in either case. Utterly cowed by the horrible spectacle of the Indian's fate, the malcontents scattered like frightened sheep. MacGregor's victory was complete.

When the party were once more seated in their comfortable quarters and Barnett's wound had been properly dressed, Sir George Sterling said : "I think we owe you our lives to-night, MacGregor."

"I believe you do," MacGregor assented. "Barnett can devise things which certainly pass the understanding of any man I ever met except himself, but there are times when a man of action is useful too."

" You have proved it," Sir George said warmly, and then he asked a question that was uppermost in the minds of all.

" Will you tell us, MacGregor, what you did to that poor devil of a savage ? "

" Nothing."

" I mean what dreadful influence or agent did you bring to bear upon him ? "

" The plate on which he stood was connected with a machine which my learned friend constructed when we first heard of the intended attack. This was done in the merciful hope, that, if driven to do it, we might, by one man's terrible fate, save many lives——espe-

cially our own. We were right in this, as you have
seen."

" But the agent employed ?"

" I cannot tell you. Barnett tried to explain its nature, but I really could not follow him. I can tell you,
however, its effect on the Indian standing on the plate
when he took hold of the metal bar."

" And that was ?"

" It almost wholly destroyed the attraction of cohesion
in the man's body."

# CHAPTER IV.

### THE STEEL GLOBE.

On the following day there was a wonderful appearance of energy and attention observable amongst the smiths and half-breeds. The Indians had vanished.

MacGregor was up and out before his guests were awake. During the day he had many consultations with Barnett and Sir George Sterling. The others idled about, smoking and talking. Rod and rifle were forgotten. The adventure of the preceding day—or night— was the only topic. There was a spot in the middle of the grass square that no one passed near, nor even looked at intentionally.

As the day advanced a strange quiet fell on the works. Before noon most of the half-breeds had passed by the hut, every man with his bundle—on tramp for the coast. There was no other destination possible to them. Now that the idlers were reminded of it they recollected having heard the captain of the coasting steamer which brought them from Vancouver Island say that his orders were to remain for a gang of workmen who were employed inland.

All day long the scowling savages passed in twos and threes. Then the less important of the smiths joined the march, so that by nightfall only a few of the skilled hands remained. These were now busily employed.

That evening the company at table was dull. This was a novel experience, but not surprising after the excitement of the previous night and its terrible tragedy. Besides, the solid men had evidently something on their minds, and the frivolous ones felt its weight vicariously. The roaring furnaces were silent. Shafts of flame no longer shot up into the smoke-laden sky. Huge rollers no longer ground the groaning bars of steel. The ponderous blows of the steam-hammer were changed to a rattle as of small arms—the busy hammers of the rivetters. Altogether a change had come. There was mystery in the air.

Several days passed, and then one morning there was absolute silence at the works. The cessation of the incessant tapping caused some languid speculation as to its meaning. Gordon, the most energetic of the junior men —as was fitting in a special correspondent—proposed to visit the works and see what had happened.

" Go yourself, like a good fellow, and tell us all about it when you come back," Blake said, lazily toying with a cigar.

The others added their excuses and petitions, so Gordon set out. In half an hour a messenger handed Blake a scrap of paper, on which was written :

"Come up, at once. It beats the 'Arabian Nights.'"

GORDON.

"Something new by that terrible Barnett," Durand said with interest; "we had better go. Come on, Graves." Blake was already hurrying up the pathway to the works.

A curious sense of impending discovery possessed the three as they walked hastily up the pathway. Blake had started first and was still slightly ahead when they came to the large rock which shut out the view of the works. An exclamation of amazement escaped him which caused the others to break into a run.

"What is it, Blake, for Heaven's sake?" Durand and Graves shouted together.

"Barnett has manufactured a—a—little moon!" Blake cried, excitedly.

There it was.

A jet black globe of steel fifty feet in diameter lay in the middle of the valley. It was almost a perfect sphere, with only a certain flattening at the top and bottom— like the polar depressions of the Earth in miniature. Barnett's work was over, his machine was made—outside and inside it was finished; the man's masterpiece was complete.

The rivetters and skilled mechanics were packing up their belongings. Theirs had been the final task of putting together all those strange castings and binders and beams of steel, every one of which fitted to the thousandth part of an inch, though wrought by men who had never seen their fellow's work.

Large as it was, it seemed a small result from all the time, and labour, and money that had been spent upon it. But Barnett had to mine for his metal; mine for his coal to smelt it; make his machinery before he made his machine; manufacture his mighty hammers as well as his hammered steel, his fierce-toothed saws as well as the plates through which they tore. He had to teach most of his workmen and oversee them all. He was constantly delayed by accidents caused by their inexperience and carelessness. His supplies were brought with enormous difficulty from the coast, or, when the ice had melted, by steamer on the great Yukon river to its nearest navigable approach to the camp, and thence overland through a mountainous country. Every imaginable obstacle had to be overcome before the work of building the steel globe could even be commenced. The Alaskan valley presented every possible disadvantage for such an enterprise, save two. These were important exceptions. One was the presence of coal and iron near the surface. The other was the absence of public opinion. The only people in that lonely valley were Barnett's friends or workmen. The former would not betray him. The latter could not; not a man of them could ever make his way back to the coast unprovided with an order to the keepers of the

various food depots which had been established at convenient intervals along the route. They would have
starved before they got half-way, had they tried to desert
before their work was finished. It was over now, and
they might tell what they pleased when they got back to
the places from which they had been drafted. Long
before that could happen the Steel Globe would have
disappeared. The Indians did not count. They never
approached civilised haunts. Besides, they did not understand. Even if they did, no one would have believed
their story. This was why Henry Barnett, after an
earnest study of the map of the world, had selected
Alaska as the scene of his strange experiment.

"Good morning, gentlemen," MacGregor shouted in his
ringing voice. He was standing close to the great black
ball. Beside him Barnett meditated in his usual abstracted
way, and hard by Sir George pencilled vigorously at those
mammoth rows of figures in his pocket ledger, adding
them, dividing them or multiplying them with perfect
correctness while simultaneously directing an animated
discourse at the solemn scientist. It is a habit easily
acquired by those who deal much with figures, and Sir
George was an adept in it.

"Come this way, please," MacGregor said, leading them
up a sloping gangway. He was followed by his bewildered friends. Through a spacious door in the side
of the globe of steel they all passed into its interior.

"You can inspect everything you wish," the guide declared, "only don't ask me any questions as to the names and uses of all these devices, for I'm hanged if I could answer you. Barnett will tell you all about them, but he has such a learned way of describing them I doubt very much if you will be anything the wiser."

A spiral staircase wound round the interior circumference of the globe. This staircase, or rather sloping path, had one very curious feature. The handrail was duplicated, so that if by any superhuman means the normous bulk could be turned upside down one could walk on the underside of the spiral as conveniently as on its upper surface. In fact, so far as appearance went, there was neither upper nor underside, the one being a perfect duplicate of the other. Again, the roof and the floor of the globe were identically fitted. Below, there were comfortable armchairs, luxurious couches, writing-tables and bookcases. Exact duplicates of these hung from above, head downwards, so to speak.

Across the centre of the Steel Globe a commodious platform swung like a ship's lamp. On this a very large telescope was fixed, and, by peering over from the spiral path, the men could see that the platform was literally packed with astronomical instruments. Strange registers, the graduated lines on which were so fine as to be almost invisible without the aid of a magnifying glass, were set into the woodwork of a solid table in the middle of the swinging deck. Strongly made iron tanks filled a considerable portion of the interior space. Each of these tanks had a register showing the state of its contents. In addition to these there was a general register which showed the state of the contents of all the tanks. These tanks contained compressed air.

Innumerable windows pierced the whole circumference of the globe. The triple plates of glass which filled everyone of these apertures were very transparent, but of great thickness and strength. It was evident therefore that the ventilation of the fabric must be accomplished by some novel arrangement. This arrangement was certainly novel in the extreme as will be seen later.

" Now you understand all about it, Blake," MacGregor said, with a laugh.

"Pretty nearly," Blake answered with pretended gravity. " There are one or two trifling details about which I am not as clear as I should like to be."

" Very probably. Still I feel sure you know as much about it as you did of the subject of your last great speech in the House."

" I am afraid I know as little about it as you do yourself, MacGregor."

" You have it exactly—all except one detail, as you would call it."

" What detail ?"

" I know where it is going. You don't."

" It ?   Where *it* is going ?   Have you sold it ? "

" Sold it !   Not to be made Grand Lama of Tibet."

" MacGregor, I think it is time we heard something about your intentions," Blake then said more seriously. " Here we have all been idling about for weeks in a primeval forest, which is distinctly more like Bedlam than Arcadia.   You, Barnett, and Sterling have some huge joke amongst you which you seem anxious to keep to yourselves.   Your nods, glances, and half sentences are very edifying, but too mysterious for ordinary life.   And now the whole thing culminates in a—curiosity "—he waved his hand towards the roof of the fabric—" that certainly beats the Eiffel Tower."

" It does," MacGregor emphatically interrupted.

" But we want to know what it means.   If you cannot tell us plainly, I'm off.   I don't want to wait for another attack from the Indians.   Nor to see another copper-skin pulverised.   Faugh ! "

" Don't be impatient, Blake, just when the mystery is about to be explained.   After dinner to-night you shall know as much as I do."

" And how much is that ? "

" I have told you already.   You shall know where it is going, and who is going inside it."

" When does it start, may I ask ? " Blake said, with a touch of sarcasm in his voice.

" To-night," was the brief reply.

"Then it is time we were preparing to evacuate the camp," Sir George said. " You, MacGregor, and Gordon, as great travellers, have only the regulation flannel shirt and pair of stockings to pack. But the rest of us like to take things more comfortably."

"What do you make of it, Durand?" Blake asked as they walked back to the hut.

"That we are leaving this interesting region to-night, and that I am not at all sorry at the prospect. I have got some good lines on these trackless forests and great glaciers. There is very little in them. It is a waste of time to remain."

"And I," said Graves, " I have got some good 'lights' amongst these pine-woods. There is nothing else to be done. I want to get back to London."

Gordon was less eager to be off. Wherever the mighty MacGregor was, on land or sea, there should the specials be gathered together, and he was thankful to have the job to himself.

But while Durand had got at least some lines, and Graves some lights, and Gordon some copy, poor Blake had got nothing. Alaska is not a fruitful field for politicians. And politicians are really sometimes—if very rarely—actuated by selfish motives.

So Blake was downcast. "Of all the monstrous absurdities I ever saw, that tremendous steel ball is *facile princeps*," he said sulkily.

"Wait till we hear what MacGregor says," Gordon remonstrated.

"Nonsense," Blake interrupted. "He is to tell us who is going inside it. Does he think we are demented? And he is to tell us where it is going. Why didn't they plant it farther up the hill, and then there would at least have been the possibility of giving it a decent roll down. It's too bad, it really is—What's this?"

A line of men carrying hampers, boxes, cases, and packages of every description came into view. These goods were at once recognised as part of Sir George Sterling's well-ordered commissariat.

"Where are you going, men?" Blake asked when they met the foremost of the train.

"To the works, sir."

"What are you to do with these cases?"

"They are for the big ball, sir."

"He is—he is—actually provisioning the ship," Blake stammered in amazement.

They walked on in silence. There was really nothing to be said. Every hour brought some new absurdity, as they thought, to light. And yet MacGregor was so practical, and so determined, and so successful in every venture of his life they could not quite bring themselves to laugh at any enterprise of his, or Barnett's.

The evening meal had never been more impatiently waited for, nor more quickly despatched. Every man was too eager for MacGregor's ultimatum to find time for an appetite. At last the time came. The explorer passed round one of Sir George's square bottles and arose. "Gentlemen," he said, " I give you as a toast—a pleasant journey and safe return to us all."

" A pleasant journey and safe return to us all," echoed pleasantly round the table, and MacGregor went on again, speaking very seriously.

"You remember that I promised you all a marvellous mission. I have to thank you for your prompt response and steadfast reliance on my sincerity. The time has come when I am able to justify the unquestioning confidence you have placed in me, and tell you whither we are bound—that is, if you are still of the same mind to trust yourselves to my venture."

" Yes, we are ! " enthusiastically.

"Thank you. I expected it. Then you are bound for the longest voyage ever men made."

" But how are we going to make it ? "

" In the Steel Globe."

A burst of angry disappointment swept round the table.

" Your humour may be very excellent, Mr. MacGregor, but you must pardon us if we consider it ill-timed," Durand said, severely.

Sir George Sterling seemed quite unmoved. He was evidently in MacGregor's confidence.

"I assure you that I consider this to be the most serious moment of my life," MacGregor answered, with a gravity that caused Blake to interject : "Sit down man, you have been drinking."

"And where on earth are we going?" they asked, derisively.

"Nowhere on earth."

"Then where, for Heaven's sake?"

There was a pause, and MacGregor said quietly :

"To the planet Mars!"

# CHAPTER V.

### A TERRIBLE VENTURE.

FOR some moments no one stirred. MacGregor's air of terrible earnestness forbade the assumption that he spoke in jest. He saw them look helplessly at each other, and said in his impetuous way : " Explain it to them, Barnett. It is only natural that they should be surprised. Tell them all about it. Describe your invention."

Barnett usually took no part in the general conversation. Like most great thinkers he was not great at small talk, notwithstanding his weakness for making a set speech. Like some profound scientists he was modest. His duty now demanded from him a service that he was well qualified to render, and he hastened to discharge it. Impressed by the solemnity of his mission, he arose in his place at the table and addressed his audience in measured terms. He had not the magical force of character owned by MacGregor. He could not by his mere personality carry men blindly with him—unquestioning, uncaring, so that they only followed. But his mighty genius was a power greater than this mysterious influence. It did not compel men to act. It convinced them that to act was right.

"I do not wonder," he said, "at your amazement. To you, MacGregor's revelation must have seemed the language of a madman. But, nevertheless, he spoke the simple truth. For twenty years I have pursued a single branch of science—not perhaps a branch, for it contains the elements of all science. It deals with the beginning of things, their continuance, their end. In this long period of research I have made many strange discoveries. The greatest of all only came to fruition about a year ago."

"I remember it well," MacGregor said, softly.

"You are all aware, of course, that the planets move in their orbits so that their periods are in the sesquiplicate ratio of their mean distances——"

"We're not," MacGregor interjected; "but go on."

"I can hardly hope to explain the whole scope of my discovery to men not acquainted with elementary scientific truths," Barnett said in a regretful tone, "but I shall endeavour to make one sublime and universal law plain to you."

He paused to consider his next words. His eager audience hardly breathed. "The great discovery of which I spoke did not come to me as a surprise," Barnett still spoke slowly. He was evidently casting about for some simple formula by which he might make his meaning clear. It was very hard to deal with men who did not even understand sesquiplicate ratios.

"For twenty years prior to that night, MacGregor, I had grasped its essence. It was only then I was able to demonstrate its application. I refer, gentlemen, to the origin and entity of force. This entity, as any scientific handbook will tell you, is all-pervading, universal, omnipotent, omnipresent. One paltry clipping of this grand secret has already been grasped by man; one local condition of it has been subordinated to his material service. In many ways it ministers to his wants, bears his burthen for him, and does his bidding with the obedience of a slave. Its generic name, electricity, is familiar to you, and is, or ought to be, terrible to all thoughtful minds. What then of the other, the dweller outside, the wilder brother which soars through all the realms of space?"

Again he paused. His thoughts crowded thick and fast upon him; but it was necessary for him to remember that he was addressing a company of men who had not studied the intricate mazes of advanced science. He resumed in glowing language:

"This wilder brother of electricity, whose essence, as I said to MacGregor, I had long grasped, is also in many of his effects, known to you all. Unasked, he carries us light and heat from the sun; he causes the stars to twinkle in the arc of night; he brings a message from the moon that bids the oceans to be moved; he bears the

earth herself on his broad bosom safely round her annual
path and whirls her once in twenty-four hours into life-
giving day and night. In his mighty grip the universe
of worlds is secure. To each he assigns a station. For
all he finds a path. He leaps from sun to sun, he flashes
from star to star. Vast and incomprehensible as are the
mysterious ways in which he moves, I have succeeded in
overmastering his grandest and yet his simplest secret."

A murmur of expectant awe broke from the trembling
listeners. Together they cried: "The secret?"

"The attraction of gravitation," Barnett answered.
"This branch of force of which I am speaking," he said
more calmly, "is as delicate as it is powerful. Once the
disturbing influence of our atmosphere—or any atmosphere—contaminates it, we have the pitiful spectacle of
a god-like force condescending to such puny tricks as
knocking down mill chimneys, deranging telegraph wires,
killing men, creating braggart thunderstorms. These, as
my experiments have proved, are but the sport of insulated waves of ethereal force. Its work is more
serious."

"But how does this affect our enterprise?" they cried.

"I am coming to that. The attraction of gravitation
is but another phase of the force which compels a needle
in Liverpool to answer the fluctuations of another in New
York. Cut the intermediate wire by which the force is
conveyed, or insulate one needle and the other ceases to

act. The space between the Earth and Mars is, as it were, one vast charged wire. Along that intangible line of communication you might send a telegram as easily as under the Atlantic Ocean. Nay, more, a body insulated from the Earth's attraction would by it pass almost instantaneously to Mars for the attraction of gravitation is inconceivably rapid. The flash of light is almost stationary beside it."

"Great heavens!"

"To-night, simply by the turning of two screws I shall insulate the Steel Globe from the Earth's attraction, and all who choose to journey by it will pass safely on to Mars."

"Instantaneously?"

"Oh, no. That would be death. My chief difficulty —indeed my only difficulty worthy of the name—has been to regulate the speed at which we travel. This I have at last accomplished. By a long series of experiments I have succeeded in graduating the counter attractions of the two planets until I can regulate our speed to a mile—or say, a thousand miles."

"And at what speed do you propose to travel?"

"Fifty thousand miles a minute," Barnett answered, and as he seated himself wearily, he said; "Mars will be in opposition in less than a month from now. For reasons which will be explained to you later, I consider it wiser to start at once."

There was a long, silent pause and then simultaneously from every throat a wild hurrah rang out. Then a bustle loud and long began ? No further questions were asked, nor doubts expressed. Barnett had already given proofs of scientific knowledge sufficient to justify the wildest scheme. Letters for home were dashed off in reckless haste. Sir George had weighty advices to despatch to his agents, brokers, and bankers. From force of habit he carefully placed his cheque-book in a convenient hand-bag. It did not strike him in the hurry of the moment that it might be difficult to cash his drafts in Mars—or that the Martian bankers might charge a ruinous commission for collecting them. Durand wrote a very passionate and sentimental farewell to his lady fair—for the time being. Graves made a hasty sketch of the scene and sent it in lieu of a letter to a brother artist somewhere in London. Gordon dashed off a paragraph for his paper in which, by stern injunction from MacGregor, no mention of the enterprise was made. And Blake wrote to his party withdrawing from a tour of political speeches they had arranged for him. MacGregor himself and Barnett did not write to any one.

All these despatches were entrusted to the late fore-man of the works, who was called into the hut and hospitably entertained before setting off on his long tramp to the coast. MacGregor, calculating on the fidelity of his party had already sent all their personal baggage to the Steel Globe. Then, for the last time, the men made their way up the pathway to where the works had been. All was in darkness; the electric lamps had been removed. No man spoke to his neighbour. The night was big with fate. Whether it should end in tragedy or farce was even yet half doubtful, but the sublimity of the possible tragedy overshadowed and suppressed the absurdity of the probable farce. There was no farce.

It was with great difficulty that the party made their way through the now silent works. Not a light burned where the garish lamps had shone, and the raging furnaces had belched forth smoke and flame, and brilliant spangles of white hot metal had flashed with vicious hisses through the grimy air. Slowly these resolute men tramped on till overhead a mighty shadow loomed higher than the dismantled sheds, blacker than the night. Then MacGregor, who led the way, turned the light of a lantern he carried on the long gangway by which entrance into the Steel Globe was gained.

"Take care how you step, gentlemen," he said; "we don't want to lose a man before the voyage begins. We may want you all before it is over."

"Reassuring, certainly," Blake grumbled, as they clambered up the gangway.

At last they were inside. A faint light flickered dismally. Its presence only deepened the general gloom.

"Bear a hand, will you?" MacGregor called to the two men nearest him. "Let's clear away this gangway." Durand and Gordon went to his assistance. In a moment the woodwork was freed and fell crashing to the ground. The entrance door was then closed by MacGregor. A massive crank was forced home, and the energetic leader said coolly:

"It may interest you all to know that we are now hermetically sealed in."

"Then how are we to breathe?"

MacGregor merely nodded in the direction of Barnett.

The latter said quietly: "The ventilation of this structure is, I believe, perfect. The surplus carbonic acid as it accumulates will be absorbed and the organic exhalations will be consumed. Fresh oxygen will be supplied from our reserves as it may be required. The tanks are gauged to emit automatically fresh air in the exact proportions necessary to health."

Barnett then stepped on the central platform and dropped into a chair with an air of familiarity which proved that this was to be his place. He immediately proceeded to strap himself into this chair with strong leather bands which were attached to its framework. The chair itself was screwed into the floor of the platform. The others huddled together on the spiral pathway.

"Gentlemen," Barnett said gravely, "you had better get as close to the top as possible. MacGregor, you will remain with me." He pointed to a second chair fitted with strong leather bands like the one in which he himself sat.

While MacGregor was strapping himself into his chair, Sir George Sterling led the way up the spiral staircase to the roof of the globe. His pocket-book with all its charm of figures was, for the moment, forgotten. They passed up till their faces almost touched the panes of triple glass, clear as the crystal of a watch but strong as hammered steel. Then they turned and looked down on the two figures below.

The man of science was calm, but the eyes of the explorer glistened. His colour was heightened. His restless blood was on fire.

"Stand clear of each other above there," MacGregor called suddenly. At the same moment Henry Barnett leaned over the table at which he sat and laid his hands on one of the curious registers before him. In this register there were two tiny screws, with an indicator like the hand of a watch attached to each. To one of these little screws he gave a delicate, hardly perceptible twist. Instantly there was a sound of tearing and crashing below. The weight of the enormous globe had gradually sunk its surface some distance into the soft ground on which it rested. The ponderous fabric was now tearing itself free from its self-made bed.

"Look out," Sir George Sterling shouted. A marvel

of marvels! The heavens and the earth were moved. The starry arc above slipped down to underneath. Constellations chased each other across the midnight sky and plunged into the ghastly gulf beneath. The mighty Earth herself towered up into a receding zenith. The milky way lay millions deep below.

"The effect you see," Sir George said in a low voice "is easily explained. It is caused by the fact that the attraction of Mars exceeded that of the Earth the moment that Barnett turned that screw. Our feet naturally point now towards the planet which has the strongest pull on us."

"Of course they do," Blake exclaimed with a gallant effort at pleasantry. "It is the simplest thing in the world. In fact I rather like it." Then with a quivering voice: "Heaven preserve us all!"

"Amen," every man was fain to add, but it was too soon to show the white feather. Nevertheless literature and art, as personified in Durand and Graves, had a commonplace look of fright. "Our own correspondent" might have belonged to anybody, and even the mighty capitalist himself had evidently weakened. Only those two maniacs on the bridge—as it might be called—bore themselves stoutly. MacGregor, indeed, was fast verging into a fever of mad exultation. Barnett was absolutely calm. He had perfected his invention—science cannot err.

So the Steel Globe continued to rise—or, as it seemed to

those within it, to fall—from the Earth's surface. Through
the upper windows could be seen a long winding silver
streak where the moonlight sparkled on the well-known
river. All else was darkness. The river itself was fast
narrowing into a fine thread of light. Already it was far
away. MacGregor came to the side of the platform and
spoke down to his followers. Five minutes before the
followers were above the platform. It had swung round
during that marvellous upheaval of all material things.
The leathern straps to the chairs on it had thus proved no
useless contrivance.

"I have a few words to say to you all and I request
your most earnest attention." MacGregor evidently spoke
under strong excitement and with something of Barnett's
measured style. He was listened to with eager interest.
He need not have anticipated any want of attention. "I
have already told you whither we are bound. Mr.
Barnett has told you how we propose to go. Now at
the last moment I feel that I ought to put it to you
whether you are willing to take the risks of this voyage."

"We have already decided," came in a hoarse chorus
from the followers.

"That is well; but you must consider again, and then
every man's life must be on his own head. Everything
that this great man of science"—pointing to Barnett—
"could do to minimise the risks of our venture has been
done, but I will not disguise from you, or myself, that

these risks are still terrible. Should my friend's calculations be at fault—of which I myself have no fear—should the atmosphere of Mars prove fatal to human life, or its inhabitants be hostile; should a meteoric body stronger than our vessel strike it; should we, in short, from any cause break down half-way, or come to grief at our journey's end, every man must accept the responsibility of his own action. The dangers surrounding our enterprise are indeed fearful. Weigh them well. On the other hand, weigh well the undying fame which awaits every man here this night if we succeed. Every man of you has been selected by me with anxious care as likely, in his own especial sphere, to render valuable service in developing the grand results of our great adventure. Believe me it was not lightly I selected men on whom I felt I could rely, not merely to face physical danger, but men to whom I could intrust an enterprise that to lesser minds must seem impious."

A murmur of approval ran through the serious group below and under the grand old explorer's impetuous words, eyes flashed and hands were clenched in gathering resolve.

"But remember that while I want a willing crew I must be captain of the ship. Barnett is now only my engineer. He simply steers the vessel. In all else I must be supreme. It is necessary for the general safety.'

"Agreed!"

" One word more." He pointed to a door in the side of the globe opposite to that by which they had entered. " That is what we have called the ejector. By a simple device of double doors any superfluous or deleterious article or—or—body can be expelled with only a trifling loss of air. Should we run short of oxygen it will be my duty to name the man who must first pass through that door."

The men below shuddered.

" If that be not enough I shall name another, and so on, till only myself and the engineer are left. Then I shall go in the hope that he may reach the end in safety, to the growth of knowledge and the advancement of science. If any man hesitates—if any man is afraid— we can still easily return to the Earth and set him free. He may never have another opportunity to go. I now require every man to accept or decline my terms."

There was another of those long silent pauses. The ghastliness of the last words MacGregor had spoken sank into the hearts of the daring adventurers, blanched their faces, and dulled their reckless spirits. But Sir George Sterling, who had most at stake—most money at stake, indeed, all the money at stake—said very quietly, and without bravado :

" I agree, and will go."

" I agree, and will go," Durand, Graves and Blake said

simultaneously, and with a certain dogged determination not to be outdone.

The correspondent sat down coolly and said nothing. It was his place to go.

" Bravo all ! " MacGregor cried effusively, as he took off his cap and saluted them. In a moment he had sprung from the platform and was running down the spiral. "I knew the stuff that made the men with whom I had to deal," he said in great delight. His courage was magnetic and gave the others fresh heart. Then in his great rasping voice he shouted up to Barnett :

" Engineer, how is the ship ? "

"Dropping at the rate of 500 feet a second. The atmosphere is now so thin we can *start* at any time."

" Can you start this moment ? "

" Certainly, I am merely holding on by a remnant of the Earth's attraction."

" You are quite ready, Barnett ? "

" Quite ready, MacGregor."

"Then—*let go !* "

## CHAPTER VI.

### AN AWFUL PLUNGE.

THE man of science had laid aside his dignity. He now acted as if under the severest discipline. You could have counted the beats of the men's hearts as he took hold of those two small screws out of all the maze of intricate mechanism before him. The one he took in his right hand, the other in his left. No mighty levers, no massive cranks! Simply two little fragile screws!

Some of those below drew a deep breath and half muttered a prayer. The engineer himself neither sighed for earth nor prayed to heaven—he was a man of science. His long white fingers did not quiver, his pulse did not increase a beat. He gave each little screw a slight turn, one this way, one that, and suddenly a fierce rush and roar of air could be heard. Barnett kept his eyes fixed on a disc before him, and thus some minutes passed. The roaring sound of rushing air grew less—then faint— and ceased.

" We are now outside the Earth's atmosphere," Barnett

said, quietly, as he gave each screw a complete turn, and then——

Down! down!

Down from the sheltering surface of the earth! Down at the rate of fifty thousand miles a minute! Down into space! The journey was begun. The silence of it! The awful and appalling silence! The thousands of constellations! The millions of stars!

A few moments after Barnett had sent the Steel Globe plunging down he pressed a button and the faint light which shone so gloomily in the ship was extinguished. Then leaving MacGregor to watch and report on the movements of the distance registers, he applied himself to the great telescope. By this time every man had stationed himself at a window to gaze at the glories of the heavens. Once the atmosphere of the Earth was passed, the many million glistening and tremulous brilliants in the sky became fixed and still, and shone with perfect steadiness in a jet black pall of space. Freed from the obscuring veil of terrestrial air, those fierce red stars, Aldebaran, 200 times as large as our great Sun himself, Betelgeux, the hugest of Orion's spheres, Antares, the Scorpion's heart, Arcturus and Pollux blazed like sunlit rubies; Capella and Procyon shed their glorious yellow beams, far surpassing the most splendid golden or topaz hues known to earth; and the brilliant glare of Altair in the Eagle and Vega in the

Lyre well-nigh rivalled the grand white sheen of mighty Sirius, threefold the brightest of all Northern stars. The planet Mars gleamed red in the constellation of the Serpent.

Delightful, too, were the contrasting tints of many other single, double, triple, or multiple stars, invisible to the unaided eye through atmospheric clouds. Twin suns, one red and its companion green, or yellow and purple, or orange and blue, lighted the inky vault of night with pyrotechnic fires, brilliant against more delicate shades of fawn, buff, lilac, silvery-white, puce, copper, and grey. Glories that the most powerful telescopes had never yet revealed were now discovered by the simplest instruments. Beauties, such as the eye of man had never yet beheld were scattered over the realms of space in bewildering loveliness. The heavens were ablaze with rainbows of the parti-coloured stars.

The Southern constellations hidden for a brief period by the mass of the Earth which blotted out the starlight in the zenith of the car came quickly into view. The vast circle of darkness grew momentarily smaller and smaller, and as it narrowed the stars crept in and in till only a measurable gap delayed the completion of the circle. The Southern Cross was soon as plainly visible as the Great Bear. Instead of an arc of a circle they were in the centre of a circle complete—a circle radiant with stellar glories undimmed by earthly atmosphere, unshorn of their gaudy colours, a thousand times more numerous, more delicate, and more bold than man could of himself conceive.

The silence was painful and yet no man spoke. At last Barnett, who was silently studying the stars through the great telescope, left it and went to his registers. These he carefully examined for some minutes, holding his watch in his hand, and glancing at it every second or two.

"Look out, below. You will see the sun in thirty seconds." He said this in his usual. quiet tones, as unmoved as if he were merely giving an opinion on the next day's weather to a farmer.

Thirty seconds! There was no sign of coming day. No ruddy flush of crimson warmed that awful vault of star-specked black. The night had soon but ten seconds more of life, and yet it did not lift its deepest pall to greet the coming day. Where was the rising of the mist from meadows, the gilding of purple hills, the rustle of the morning breeze, the gentle sighing of leaf-laden trees, the matin-song of thanksgiving birds? And yet what had these harbingers of sunrise on the Earth to do with sunrise on the road to Mars—with dawn in space?

Five seconds more, and but for the stars a darkness so thick that well-nigh it might be felt. Then a great shout rang out:

"The Sun!"

And from behind the fast decreasing shadow of the Earth, the Sun himself leaped forth. The practical solar eclipse which had so far obtained might have lasted longer but for the plan already decided on by Barnett. He had started from weighty reasons when Mars was within a month of opposition; consequently the journey of the Steel Globe was not a direct line from the Sun to Mars although it was an absolutely direct line from the Earth to that planet. Owing to this, the Sun emerged from the side of the Earth's shadow before that shadow would have become small enough to discover him had the voyagers journeyed in a direct line.

And now a strange thing happened. While without the heavens held unchanged their diamond-spangled gloom, within, the steel ship flashed from midnight into high noon. The sunlight which pierced in a long un-broken shaft through the vast emptiness of space burst through the windows of the globe and, mingling with its interior atmosphere, softened and suffused into an earthly day. Marvellous contrast! Within, a sunny summer's day; without, a universe in solemn night! and the Sun, encircled by his grand corona, glaring like a fierce, un-blinking beacon, was only brighter than any of the other myriad multi-coloured suns—a star himself, that in his glory differed only in degree from the glory of other stars.

## CHAPTER VII.

### SAILING THROUGH SPACE.

As the bright light swept through the ship, every passenger in it turned to look in his neighbour's face and see how he fared. And every man was startled to see the wan white face that met his own. The excitement had told on all. Even the indomitable MacGregor showed traces of it. Barnett went on placidly with his observations and remained at the telescope for several hours.

How readily one grows accustomed to novel surroundings! In a couple of hours the adventurers had recovered their usual spirits, and were coolly settling down to while away the voyage. Gordon sketched out a grand descriptive article for his paper. Durand and Graves carried on an animated discussion on sidereal "lights" and "lines." Blake had already made progress with the preparation of a powerful address to the Martian Senate, in which he proposed administering some crushing oratorical blows to their form of government —if they had any. And Sir George Sterling was so

far recovered as to feel able to take an interest in
figures.

About six hours slipped away without any change.
Nearly twenty millions of miles had flashed past with
hardly a breath to tell their story, nor even a sign to
mark their trail. Sometimes, indeed, the dead silence
of the journey was broken by a startling crash as the
Steel Globe plunged through a rush of meteors, exploding
them in its headlong flight like a *feu-de-joie*. Without,
the stillness of space was doubtless undisturbed by these
aërolites, but within the vibrating atmosphere of the
globe bewailed their destruction. The planet Mars
became perceptibly brighter to the naked eye. The
Earth was but a brilliant star. Then Barnett took
charge of the registers from MacGregor.

" Now that we are about half-way across," the captain
of the ship said pleasantly, as he descended the spiral
stairway, " I propose supper."

" Are you serious, MacGregor ? " Sir George asked.
The baronet, like all good Englishmen, appreciated a
sirloin better than a sermon, but at the moment his
appetite was far from keen.

"Of course I am serious. Pull out that hamper, Blake."

Blake pulled a hamper from beneath a heap of books
and baggage and opened it.

" Give me that utensil," MacGregor said, as Blake, to
his own astonishment, turned out a neat brass kettle.

"What, in the name of all that's marvellous, do you want with a kettle?"

"To boil water in, curiously enongh," MacGregor answered, with an affectation of friendly superiority.

"Oh, of course! How stupid of me not to think of it! Any other little surprises?" Blake remarked, a little snappishly.

"By-and-by, perhaps. Have patience."

By this time MacGregor had filled the kettle with cold water from a jar. Whereupon he ran up the spiral, and having unlocked a plate in the side of the Steel Globe, he placed it in a small recess. This done, he closed the plate, relocked it, and returned to his party below.

Meanwhile Sir George took charge of the preparations for the feast. Under his direction, a snow-white cloth was spread on the largest of the tables; knives, forks, plates, and all the paraphernalia of a comfortable and even luxurious repast were laid on it—laid, not pitched about anyhow, for the baronet prided himself on his knowledge of gastronomic amenities. From the hamper in due succession came a long array of the good things which he had brought from London, and a couple of the square bottles were also placed upon the board. In addition, fresh fish and game, cold but nicely cooked and appetising, made their appearance.

"Barnett, you will drink tea, I know."

" Yes, thank you, Sir George," Barnett answered from above among his registers.

MacGregor made another journey up the spiral, and the hinged plate was again unlocked. He wrapped his hand in a napkin and straightway produced the kettle which was steaming merrily.

" Well I'm——"

Blake stopped and looked helplessly at Durand, who in turn looked helplessly at MacGregor. He seemed to enjoy his mystery.

" Now, MacGregor, none of your conjuring. The whole business is sufficiently out of the common already," Durand remonstrated.

" My dear fellow, it does not require a conjurer to boil a kettle, does it ? "

" It wants a bit of conjuring to boil it by simply sticking it in a hole in the wall," Blake remarked.

" Pooh, pooh ! I merely placed the kettle against the outer skin of the car."

" How simple ! Almost any of us could do that," Graves said placidly.

He took little interest in the matter. There is nothing artistic in culinary operations.

" Are any of you aware of what the sun's heat on the outside of this car, now that we have no atmosphere to protect us, amounts to ? " MacGregor asked.

" We're not," Blake promptly admitted.

"Well it—well, in fact, neither am I. What is it, Barnett?"

"About 300 degrees Fahrenheit."

"The devil it is," Blake exclaimed, as he sprang from the side of the car near which he had been standing.

"You need not be alarmed, the outside of the car might be white hot and you would not know it here."

MacGregor, as usual, nodded towards Barnett, inferring that the man of science had provided for all contingencies.

"But now for supper. Some of you fetch Barnett his tea. It is quite ready. After we have had our food we shall make a brew of whisky punch."

Sir George, though doubtful at first, notwithstanding the interest he took in the preparations for the meal, found his appetite grow, as it were, by what it fed on. MacGregor was heartily hungry, so the two set a healthy example, which was followed at a long distance, certainly, by the younger men. Graves, indeed, under any circumstances, only regarded a meal as a sort of solid foundation for a pipe, and, as smoking was not allowed, the feast had little attraction for him. Durand, Gordon, and Blake ate somewhat better; but to all it was surely a strange situation—a well-appointed table in an inter-planetary ship, speeding along, out twenty million miles in space.

After dinner, Blake said with a slight yawn:

"Now, Durand read us some of your last poetry, or tell us your last plot. It will pass the time."

Thirteen hours only from the Earth to Mars, and here was a growl at the length of the voyage!

"What shall I read?" Durand asked, with well-affected indifference.

"Oh, it's all the same. I don't know one of your pieces from another; it's only to pass the time, you know."

"Indeed!" Durand tried hard to appear unconcerned, and was quite as successful as might have been the mother of a slighted first-born prodigy. Literary men have sometimes declared they actually forget the names of their own characters when writing a book. But they are only fibbing when they say so, or they have been writing quite shockingly bad stories.

Blake hastily tried to repair his error. "I mean, there is so much—so much spirit in everything you write; anything of yours will keep us going."

But Durand was not pacified, and there were no readings. An unsuccessful attempt was made to lure Barnett into one of his didactic speeches, but it also failed. The scientist was too busy to permit himself even the luxury of a lecture. So for six or seven hours more there was nothing to do but watch the stars. No one thought of sleep, although for nearly twenty-four hours they had been awake. Conversation was kept up in feverish snatches, not so much for any interest in the subject discussed as to relieve the nervous strain which pressed more heavily as the time passed by, and the end of this wild journey drew ever nearer.

What would the end be? Mars fast grew brighter and larger. Its disc was visibly increasing in size. It was no longer a star. It was a miniature moon. Then Barnett spoke.

"The registers have proved beautifully exact. We are within a million miles of Mars."

"Will you slow down now?" came in a breathless murmur from the passengers.

"Oh no. Our oxygen is lasting splendidly, but we must be prepared for all contingencies and lose no time."

"What contingencies?"

"The possibility, for instance, of having to return to the Earth without being able to renew our supply of air."

"Ah! Are you quite sure of your distance, sir?" Blake asked timidly.

"Quite sure, Mr. Blake. It would not do to make a mistake."

"I should think not, sir. But—but—if we hit Mars at this rate we should make rather a hole in it, should we not?"

"We could not hit Mars at this rate."

"Why not, sir?"

"If we entered the atmosphere of Mars at this rate, the heat generated by the friction would cause this car and all it contains to ignite and pass into vapour."

" Ahem! That's very nice," Blake said blankly as he turned to his companions. Then, seeing their faces become suddenly grave, he said in a hesitating voice:

"I beg your pardon, Mr. Barnett,—but—don't you think it might be well to slow down—say twenty or thirty thousand miles a minute."

A smile passed over the rueful faces as Blake stammered out his request, with all its indifference to an odd ten thousand miles a minute.

"There is nothing to fear," Barnett replied, "except perhaps——"

"Perhaps what?"

"I may have miscalculated the power of the earth's attraction at the distance of fifty millions of miles. But that is unlikely."

"But suppose you have, sir; what then?"

"Well—we should not be able to slow down."

"And we'll hit Mars at the rate of fifty thousand miles a minute?"

"We shall enter the atmosphere of Mars at that rate," Barnett ominously corrected.

"That is certainly cheerful." Blake muttered.

"MacGregor, please come up here," the scientist said. "And you, gentlemen, had better all lie down and hold on to something. The car may oscillate when we strike the atmosphere of Mars, not at the rate Mr. Blake fears," he added, smiling pleasantly.

All lay down as directed. MacGregor mounted to the platform. He and Barnett strapped themselves into their seats.

"MacGregor, you must watch the duplicate, and call out the distance by it when we come within two hundred thousand miles of Mars. My attention must not be taken from the main register for the twentieth part of a second."

"Very well," MacGregor said firmly. "Shall I repeat the distances?"

"Yes, call every fifty thousand miles."

This instruction was listened to by the men below with beating hearts. Now the time of their great trial was come. It was worse than the first—worse than when they had plunged down from the Earth.

"Two hundred thousand miles from Mars," MacGregor called in a hard impassive voice. He had braced himself to his task. His face was rigid. It was almost through his clenched teeth that he spoke.

"Right!" Barnett answered, his eyes fixed on the main register. He laid his right hand on one of the little screws, his left hand on the other.

"Hundred and fifty!"

"Right!"

A circle of light began to blot the heavens out below. The huge circumference of Mars widened with every passing second. He stretched forth his great arms of fire and clutched at the flying stars.

"Hundred!"

"Right!"

MacGregor's tones were hoarse, but Barnett's voice rang clear as a bell. His right hand turned gently towards his left; his left hand turned towards his right. Ah! great Mars, your giant size grows not now so fast. The Steel Globe had slackened pace by one-half its full velocity.

"Fifty!"

"Right!"

MacGregor's voice was now a gasp. The men below shut their eyes as though they fain would shut out that ever growing spectral world beneath.

Another turn of those tiny screws! Ah, if one slight thread should snap or clog!

Four times more MacGregor called the distance and Barnett replied. Then the man of science twisted home his screws and left the platform with MacGregor.

"Now, gentlemen," Barnett said as he joined the group below, "we shall enter the denser atmosphere of Mars in twenty-five seconds."

"At what rate?" cried all.

"About one thousand feet a second—a speed not so great as to give any grounds for apprehension."

A cry of gratitude and deep emotion went up that sounded like a congregational Amen.

"Is it quite safe to leave the—to leave those registers, Mr. Barnett?"

"It would be useless for me to remain above," Barnett answered.

"Not useless, surely?"

"Yes, for the attraction of Mars is now shut off, and that of the Earth full on. I can do no more."

And then before another man could speak the Steel Globe passed into the denser atmosphere of Mars amid the shrieking welcome of ten thousand storm fiends begotten of its own fierce force. But the resistance of the air quickly arrested the rapidity of its progress, and it sank to the surface of the planet, and rested upon it with a shock no greater than that of a shunting locomotive.

So after that wild sail through fifty million miles of space these pioneers of science had safely reached their harbour. Whether human life existed on Mars or was possible on it, whether it should prove a world of welcome or a dance of death, a triumph or a sepulchre, no man yet knew.

# CHAPTER VIII.

### THE PLANET MARS.

"IT *is* possible to breathe this atmosphere;" so spake Henry Barnett.

"Thank God!"

"Yes, you see this phial. It was exhausted a minute ago. It is now filled with Martian air. I have tested it by a process over which I spent many weeks of careful experiment. It is somewhat rarer than the air which we find most comfort in breathing but not so rare as to be deleterious."

"You are quite sure, Mr. Barnett, that it is Martian air you have got in the bottle."

"Certainly, it could be nothing else. That tube through which I filled it was specially constructed for this purpose.

"MacGregor—*you may open the door.*"

"Bear a hand with these levers," MacGregor shouted cheerfully. In a few moments the powerful bolts and bars on the main side-door were withdrawn, the door was opened, and a rope-ladder lowered down which all clambered and set their feet on the planet Mars.

"And is *this* Mars?"

Well might the bitter exclamation pass from lip to lip. Was this what they had done and dared so much to see? Was this sorrowful wilderness the reward of a venture more gallant and audacious than ever man had yet achieved. Was this all?

A boundless plain of fine red sand stretched round them as far as the horizon on every side, east, west, north, south. In this dead waste there was neither hill nor dale, mountain nor lake, nor bird nor beast. Neither was there any living thing whatsoever, animal or vegetable; not a shrub, not a leaf, nor even a blade of humblest herbage upon it, and over it a dull red sky hung gloomily, unstirred by a breath of wind, unrustled by the pinion sweep of birds—a fitting landscape for the well-named planet Mars, the god of war, desolation, and death.

"Barnett, where are we?" MacGregor asked in a broken voice. Despair had hold of him.

"Pshaw, man," Barnett said more sharply than was usual with him; "you did not expect to find life in the great equatorial continents of Mars, unwatered for thousands of years."

"Then you have some general idea of where we are?"

"I have a very precise idea that we are in South

latitude fifteen degrees. I can't tell you our longitude for I do not know where to place the Martian meridian. But I can, at least, tell you that we are not far from the centre of the Secchi continent."

Barnett's undismayed spirit helped to restore confidence to the failing hearts of his companions. Sir George and MacGregor stood close to him while he worked out some calculations based on observations already made. Durand, Graves, Blake and Gordon moved apart in a silent group. They had fallen into this habit of separation in moments of extreme crisis. At such times it seemed right that the directors of the enterprise should be left to themselves.

It was almost impossible to walk in the soft fine sand. Besides, every footstep stirred up little clouds of it which rose in blinding wreaths, and filled their eyes, ears, and nostrils. There was no protection against its penetrating particles. It was everywhere; irritating and inflaming every pore.

A curious change had come over the appearance of the Steel Globe. When it left the earth it was jet black. Now it was slate grey all over. In places it was dented deep and scarred. Great weals rose upon it here and there. Portions of its surface seemed charred and scorched. It had not passed scatheless through the countless swarms of meteors that everlastingly soar through the lonely wastes of space.

A cry from Gordon who had moved off alone from the

second group attracted the attention of his party. Possessed of an inquiring mind—or on the look-out for copy—he was always dodging about in out-of-the-way places, note-book in hand.

"Come here, come here!" he cried so excitedly that his three companions ran up.

"By heaven! the globe is sinking into the sand," they all exclaimed together.

"MacGregor, Barnett, Sterling, run for your lives."

The Steel Globe was fast sinking into a dry quicksand. Ten feet of its bulk had already disappeared.

The leaders ran to the spot as quickly as the cumbering sand would permit. A long trail like red smoke followed in their wake.

"Jump in, jump in," MacGregor shouted, leading the way himself.

"I think it ought to be 'jump out, jump out,'" Blake exclaimed. "The whole thing will be under sand in five minutes."

"You need not hurry," Barnett said quietly. "It is certainly better to get inside before the sand is up to the door. But that is all you need trouble about."

"Of course if you are sure of being able to raise the ship," MacGregor began apologetically, but Barnett interrupted.

"Raise the ship, MacGregor! If the steel frame

would hold together I could tear that ship from the centre of Mars."

They listened to him and believed him like children. His word was law unto them. Standing in a group by the door they watched the sand rise slowly up foot by foot. They hardly spoke at all. Sometimes from sheer weariness they raised their eyes from the flat sea of sand. But no variegated clouds relieved the dull glare of the lurid sky, no snowy banks of dazzling fleece, pierced by shafts of azure, brightened the sombre pall through which the Sun, diminished to two-thirds hts disc as seen from the Earth, glared sickly. The solitude was intense, oppressive. Beside it all the earthly loneliness that any man had known was mirth and laughter. Nothing upon the living Earth could compare in horror with the silent, ghastly death of that great Secchi continent in dead or dying Mars.

The silence was broken suddenly by a long wailing moan. It came from the North, and with terrific speed screamed phantom-like overhead; then died away South-wards in a dreary sob. A rush of air whirled madly in the track of that wild shriek, ploughing a weird furrow in the desert sand, searing it as with the blistering trail of a demon. But nothing visible passed by.

With a shudder the men sprang to Barnett : " What was that ? "

" I cannot say," he answered seriously, almost solemnly.

"Have you any way of getting out of this—this valley of death?" Sir George asked blankly.

"Oh, yes."

"Then why do you wait? It is terrible."

"Wait? I am waiting for a breeze."

"For which you will wait till doomsday," the younger men broke out impetuously.

"Not at all. I shall not wait an hour."

"Pardon me, Mr. Barnett, but how do you know?" Durand said in a firm but respectful voice. Every one was respectful to Barnett. Of course they were more or less respectful to each other. But there was a touch of awe in their voices when they spoke to the scientist. At the same time they had had enough of mystery—enough and to spare.

"Why, look at the sky."

"It's a treat I must say," Blake muttered.

"It is full of sand. There is a strong wind up there. We shall have it presently."

The gloomy sky grew darker still. On the horizon a deep cloud gathered.

"We shall have the wind immediately, and from the right quarter," Barnett said gladly. "In, now, and close up."

All felt this change to be a relief and busily assisted. When the great central door was clamped up Barnett touched his screws. The Steel Globe rose from the devouring grip of the hungry quicksand, and soared upward like a balloon. At the altitude of half a mile the engineer put to the test the greatest marvel of his invention. By the beautiful counterpoise of contrasting mechanism he succeeded in exactly balancing the attraction and repulsion of Mars, so that the altitude of half a mile neither increased nor diminished.

"Now," said Barnett, "it only remains for us to watch the planet as we drift south. This north-westerly wind will drive us towards the De la Rue or Dawes ocean. If Mars is inhabited it will be in those regions." He went to his instruments again and after a careful examination said : "I think it is probable that we shall pass over the Lagrange peninsula. We must watch it closely. It is more favourably situated for animal life than any other portion of the planet."

The Steel Globe was now floating fast before a strengthening gale. It was useless to level field-glasses on the plain beneath, for a thick sand-cloud shut off all sight of it. Barnett watched the swirling sea of sand for some time with evident curiosity; then he said decidedly :

"It is as I expected."

"I should be very much surprised if it were otherwise—whatever it may be," Blake ejaculated.

"What are you about now, Barnett?" MacGregor asked, ever eager for fresh discovery.

"I am convinced that the canals which Schiaparelli

observed from Milan in '77 are in reality simooms crossing the great central continents of Mars. If he was observing Mars at this moment he would draw a canal in his chart in the exact course we are travelling."

"Well, I am not an astronomer," MacGregor remarked, "but surely I remember that Schiaparelli observed these same canals in '79 and '81."

"Why not? These winds may be—must be—as regular as our trades."

"How stupid of me! I forgot that," Macgregor admitted.

"I should not like to be down there now," Sir George Sterling observed. "Look at the curling wreaths of that frightful sand."

"I should think you would not come back to describe it. Talk of simooms! There's never a camel could breathe in that for five minutes. Gordon, make a note of it."

"It's down already," Gordon said shortly. He disliked being instructed in his own business.

Graves and Durand looked out listlessly. The feeling of motion was at least more agreeable than the long wait which had damped their ardour so much. But there were neither lights nor lines to be got out of that sombre sea of drifting sand. There was so far nothing in Mars but monotony—unrelieved monotony, neither light nor shade, leafy dell nor surging sea, cliff nor cavern; no gorgeous colours, nor soft tints, nor strange people, nor any people whatever. For literature and art there was practically nothing in it.

Sir George Sterling was also depressed. The syndicate outlined in that bulky pocket-book was likely to remain for ever in its pages. Who would pay the ransom of a king to visit a lonely desert of blood-red sand? Blake, usually the most talkative, was morose and silent.

Barnett rarely troubled himself about the humours of his fellow-travellers. It was his part to invent, to design. Let the rest sustain each other. But now he was moved by the general dejection.

"Why, gentlemen, you are strangely downcast. I thought we were all agreed not to expect to meet with life in the equatorial deserts of Mars."

"Might we ask, Mr. Barnett," Blake said dolefully, "do you expect to meet with life anywhere in Mars, or anything but this dreadful sandstorm?"

"Most certainly."

There was a general murmur of interest, and Barnett repeated:

"Most certainly I do, but not here. By a little extra trouble I might have struck the planet in any degree of latitude I chose, and so have saved this delay, but I was well satisfied to get a landfall anywhere."

"And you must admit he landed you in a soft place," MacGregor interposed jocularly.

"Faith, it was nearly too soft. We don't mind the delay, Mr. Barnett, if you think it is not all like this."

"I *know* it is not all like this," Barnett said, so positively that hope began to revive.

"Thank you, Barnett," MacGregor whispered, "I am glad you spoke to them."

The gale continued all day, and when night fell it had not abated. Barnett turned on his electric light and the Steel Globe looked more cheerful when pleasantly illuminated.

"Are we still driving south?" MacGregor asked, as the darkness without became intense.

"Yes, and very fast—I am afraid dangerously fast—fully forty miles an hour."

"Well, that is not unreasonable, considering that we have travelled fifty thousand miles a minute in the same ship."

"It is much more dangerous, considering the altered conditions."

"How so?"

"Before there was at least nothing serious in the way. If we strike a mountain range at this rate, we shall be nearly as badly off as if we had verified Mr. Blake's fears. It will not be as tremendous a collision, but it will be sufficient."

"Merciful powers! are we never to be free from these outlandish risks?" Blake exclaimed. It must not be sup-

posed that he was one whit more afraid than his comrades.

But he usually acted as spokesman for the junior party
owing to his greater readiness of expression. This
fluency he had gained in his training as a political speaker,
during which he had frequently, at very short notice, to
describe his views on dozens of new subjects—sometimes
his dozen of new views on the same subject.

"But, Mr. Barnett," the troubled politician asked,
"would not this attraction of gravity business of yours—
which I must say beats anything imaginable—lift us over
a mountain range?"

"Yes, provided I knew when to increase our altitude"

"I thought the machine would increase its own altitude
automatically."

"In what way?"

"I'm not able to describe it scientifically. But I
thought that we would always keep exactly half a mile
above the surface of the earth—of Mars I mean."

"No. Precisely half a mile further from the centre
of Mars than the surface below us. A mountain five
thousand feet in height would be an awkward obstacle."

"Then I give it up, sir," Blake said disconsolately.
"If that is the arrangement I really don't see why you
should not let the ship rise ten or twelve miles and relieve
our minds."

"There are three reasons," Barnett replied with calm

decision. He was not egotistical, but his supreme self-confidence was sometimes rather irritating.

"First, because we should lose our breeze, which would not suit us. Second, because we should be obliged to expend our own supply of oxygen, which also would not suit us. A rarer atmosphere than the strata we are now in would be useless. And third, because I don't believe there are any mountains hereabouts."

"Why didn't you say that before?" Blake was about to retort, but he checked himself.

"At the same time," Barnett continued, "I am always anxious that you should know exactly what I am doing. The feeling of responsibility would otherwise distract my attention from necessary observations."

"Don't trouble yourself, Barnett," MacGregor said," we all know we are in good hands. It won't be your fault if an accident happens. You might lower the light and let these fellows get to sleep. They need a rest."

"We do. We need it badly," Blake assented.

The folding-chairs and couches were arranged and all but Barnett and MacGregor lay down. Gordon, like a good traveller, was asleep in a moment. Blake dropped off in the middle of a visionary address to his constituents. Durand and Graves shook hands with unusual warmth of feeling after all they had passed safely through. And Sir George devoutly read a few pages of his pocket ledger before stretching himself out to rest.

Soon they were all breathing heavily and dreaming, according to their various natures, of special articles, great speeches, marvellous romances, gorgeous pictures, monstrous profits.

Barnett touched a button and the electric light was reduced to a faint glimmer. Then he and MacGregor, both haggard and white from long-sustained excitement, kept watch and ward on the platform, while below, the resting sleepers, in airy fancy, balanced ponderous ledgers, or wrote immortal essays, or watched the far Earth's dreamland faces softly come and go.

A faint wail came from the far South. Again that strange wild sound swept past, but not so close as before, and moaned away to silence in the North. The two sentinels clasped each other's hands.

" There it is again ! "

" Barnett, can you make anything of it ? "

" No, MacGregor. It is beyond me. It is very terrible."

# CHAPTER IX.

## PARADISE !

" HOLD on, Barnett, I see a city ! "

The slumberers sprang to their feet, awakened by MacGregor's strident tones. Eager faces thronged to the windows, and field-glasses were levelled towards the surface of Mars.

What a transformation from the previous night !

The fierce air-serpent that had twisted in its sinuous, undulating folds of blinding sand had vanished. The lurid pall of sky had been rolled back. On high the sun shone nobly in a glorious span of cloudless blue. To the south the verdure-covered mountains of the Lagrange peninsula appeared in wavy lines of grand symmetric curves. Nearer, the silvery waves of the Maraldi sea splashed pleasantly into rocky inlets, and tumbled in mimic breakers over yellow sands that shone like gold in the morning light. To the east other seas, other mountains, vast plains covered with luxuriant vegetation, sweeping, flower-decked hills, terraces of swelling green, brilliant with myriads of gaudy blossoms, beautiful trees, waving feathery foliage over countless swarms of happy song-birds, strains of distant music borne upward on the faint morning zephyr and blending with the slow murmur of the sporting waves, and there, on the shores of Pratt bay, an arm of the Maraldi sea, a great glare of marble covered the land for many miles!

In silence they watched the scene while Barnett lowered the ship till with the distant music there mingled the chorus of all the thousand warblers of the woods, the babbling of many purling streams, the unfamiliar calls of strange and gentle beasts, the busy hum of insect life. And through the now open windows, sweet flowers breathed up their perfumed sighs, and bathed the enchanted travellers in a mystic spell of delight, exquisitely sensuous but absolutely pure. Their grand adventure had not failed. The terrible ordeal through which they had passed had brought its reward, and every weary traveller reverently exclaimed:

" Paradise ! "

At that word Henry Barnett's head sank down upon his breast. With a calm smile of great content he muttered: " The battle's won, MacGregor," and fainted away.

" Ay, and well won, brave heart," MacGregor cried, as he sprang to Barnett's assistance.

In a few minutes the engineer was partially restored, and MacGregor felt at liberty to administer a reproof to him after the manner of those wise persons in the humbler classes who chastise a child for injuring itself by accident.

" You must not indulge in luxuries of that kind again, Barnett. We could not spare you yet. There is still much to be done."

" MacGregor's frankness is quite charming," Blake said pointedly.

It was indeed rather an ungracious expression of sympathy; but MacGregor had the sublime egoism of a born leader, and, like all great captains, he never reckoned those in his command as more than factors for the furtherance of his own objects, to which end he spared neither himself nor them. Of course he had a weaker, less selfish, non-professional side to his character. But this was sternly subordinated, and treated as a mere dissipation which must be sparingly indulged.

When Barnett had recovered his full strength he said : " This gentle breeze will just waft us over the city. We shall descend in the middle of it."

" Would it not be safer to run down here ? " Sir George Sterling said. He was examining some object in the landscape through a strong glass, for Barnett had been obliged to increase their altitude to cross a range of hills. " I see a villa right below. There is a machine like an enormous telescope pointed at us."

" Look ! There are the people ! " MacGregor shouted.

It was true. The telescope which Sir George saw was really pointed at the drifting globe, and curiously but very beautifully dressed beings were evidently watching the progress of the air-ship.

"That decides me," Barnett said. "I shall descend when we are exactly overhead. These will be people of education. We shall be safe with them."

"Safe! are we ever to be safe? What is wrong now, Mr. Barnett?" Blake asked.

"Nothing, I hope, but if any of the inhabitants are unenlightened—which is very unlikely—we might create a panic by this uninvited visit."

"Why do you think it unlikely that any of the inhabitants should be unenlightened, Mr. Barnett?"

"From what we have seen of the planet in the Secchi continent."

"Pray don't remind us of that."

"And also what we see of it here."

"It is delightful here, but I can't understand what that has to do with the general inhabitants, Barnett," Sir George broke in. "We landed in a howling wilderness; we arrive at an earthly, or a Martian, paradise. What more?"

"Much more. In the Secchi continent I came to the conclusion that all the equatorial regions of the planet were dead, and I was right. At one time I feared the whole planet might be in a similar state."

"You did not say so," Blake interjected.

"I did not think it judicious," Barnett drily answered. "Here I find further evidence of the old age of Mars, if I may so describe it."

"Old age! It is grand—glorious—a dream of beauty," cried all.

"It is beautiful, but it is not grand," Barnett went on, in his didactic style. "The beauty is the quiet and indeed surpassing loveliness of material perfection. The next stage will be decay. Look at those sloping mountains worn with the storms of ages. There are no gaunt cliffs upon their sweeping summits. Their sides are clad with flowers. They are beautiful, but they have not the rugged grandeur of our geologically youthful Alpine crags. That shimmering sea, plashing a lullaby on its smooth, time-worn shores is very beautiful to look upon, but it has long lost the wrathful elements of an ocean's grandeur. It is shallow; it is a mere lake. It was a mighty sea thousands of years before our Atlantic had been evolved from chaotic elements. Rude and hardy vegetation has everywhere, as you see, been supplanted by delicate growths. Those charming shrubs are but pigmies beside our forest monarchs. Those pretty and very wonderful animals are delicately shaped, but see how sensitive they are to the slightest sound, or breath of air —a thousand of them would not face a tiger. I tell you, gentlemen, the planet Mars is old. The inhabitants that

we shall find upon it will be creatures far surpassing ourselves in every attribute of mind and body. They will
have developed social, moral, and physical conditions
such as we cannot imagine. They are at the pinnacle
of their perfection. Before them there is no further
progress. Their only change must be towards decay."

Fired by scientific enthusiasm, Barnett's grave eyes
flashed, and his pale face flushed as he worked out his
grand induction. It was time to test it, the ship was
directly over the villa Sir George had discovered.

"Now we shall put my theory to the proof; there are
wonders in store for us all."

"We have had our share already," the ever-critical
Blake commented.

Barnett's thesis was sublime, but the first step towards
its demonstration was ridiculous. As he went up to
adjust his registers, and let the ship descend, his audience
returned to the windows and watched the telescope which
was still pointed towards them.

"It may be a telescope, but to me it looks uncomfort-
ably like a big gun," Blake said to his three particular
friends.

"That is just what we think of it," Durand replied.

"What a nuisance if after all that dear old Barnett
has done, they should knock the bottom out of his ship at
the last moment," Graves the silent remarked carelessly.

This member of the party spoke so seldom, it was generally presumed that he thought deeply.

"It would be extremely awkward for you, too, don't you think?" Blake asked, slightly nettled at the unnatural coolness of the artist, which he believed to be affected.

"Not so bad as for Barnett."

"Why not?"

"The ship's not mine," Graves answered.

"Oh, rubbish!"

"Let us show a white flag," some one said.

"White may be their colour of defiance," said others.

"Then a black flag, a blue flag, any sort of flag, rather than make no sign at all!"

The machine below moved slowly to and fro, as though whoever was directing its movements wished to bring it exactly in line with the descending globe.

Barnett looked down anxiously. Their altitude was now only about five hundred feet, and that distance was steadily lessening. At three hundred feet the Steel Globe stopped with a jerk. The engineer ran to his registers. For the first time he was puzzled. The indicators, which ought to show at what rate the car rose or fell, pointed exactly as they had done a moment before: but the car itself was stationary. Barnett thought for a moment, made one or two experiments with his registers, and then said angrily:

"They know as much as I, and their mechanism is more powerful."

"What is wrong?"

"They have insulated the attraction of the planet on our ship. Oh, heaven!"

"Barnett, what is it?"

The engineer turned a face of blank despair to them and said slowly: "They have cut off their own attraction. When they can do this, they must surely know how to exert their repellent force." Then, with the first faint-hearted accents that had ever fallen from him, he said, "They may shoot us into the Sun at any moment."

MacGregor seized a parachute which hung ready for use, and shouted: "Help me with the door."

"Take care, MacGregor, they could shoot you into the Sun as easily as the car itself."

"I'll chance it. Heave on that lever."

The massive door was forced open, and with a great spring the captain left his ship.

The parachute was of a new construction. It opened in the first few feet of fall, and MacGregor soared safely down to within fifty feet of the ground. Then he, too, stopped.

It was an awkward dilemma. The explorer had been in many very awkward dilemmas before; but nothing quite so bad as this. For a moment or two he appeared to review his position. Then he gave way to alarm, and kicked about vigorously as he saw the distended hood of the parachute close in, limp and relaxed. There was no longer any pull upon it to keep it open. MacGregor did not now weigh an ounce.

"Oh, come now, this is too much. Let me down. I can't kick about here all day," he shouted lustily, forgetting that it was hardly possible that the people below understood the English language (spoken with a strong Scotch accent) and that he himself did not know the alphabet of Lagrange.

"Hallo, MacGregor, how do you feel?" Blake called down, unable to suppress a laugh, for poor MacGregor did not look to advantage.

"What is that to you?" MacGregor shouted savagely; "you would not laugh if you were here."

"I beg your pardon, MacGregor," Blake said penitently, "I am as sorry as I can be, but——" Another and general laugh, in which the grave engineer joined, to the further rage of the wrathful captain.

"It's really a shame, MacGregor," Blake said; "but if you could only see yourself with all that graceful drapery."

"To the devil with it," Macgregor blurted out viciously as he shook off the parachute, in the cloth of which he was ludicrously enveloped.

"Shall we lower a rope, MacGregor?" Sir George asked; "you may as well come up again."

"What would be the use of it? I don't believe they would let it down to me." Then he shouted passionately : "Below there! Can't you let me down. What on earth do you mean—that is, what on Mars do you mean by it? We don't want to hurt you. We don't indeed."

His last words were spoken more gently, and were accompanied by gestures of pathetic appeal. These gentler actions succeeded where his wildest kicks had failed. MacGregor suddenly felt his descent recommence —and remembered that he had let go the parachute.

# CHAPTER X.

## A STRANGE VISION.

MACGREGOR made a desperate clutch at the parachute, but it was fixed in the air, and above his reach. A shudder passed through the circle of his friends above. They turned away their faces from the cruel spectacle which they dreaded to behold. A minute ago they were jesting and laughing; and now, unless a miracle should happen, the hairbreadth escapes of their daring leader were over, and his mutilated body would be only a sad souvenir of his courage.

Something very like a miracle did happen. To his own intense surprise and great relief, MacGregor felt himself sink gently down to Mars at an agreeably easy rate. Indeed, when his feet touched ground, he scarcely staggered, so carefully had his course been guided by the mysterious power at work. Once landed, he turned and waved his hand joyfully to the men above, whose spirits underwent a pleasant revolution. This leniency was surely friendly in the men of Mars. Their power might have been employed differently and with terrible consequences, had they chosen to exercise it.

MacGregor was not long in effecting his own introduction. From the ship, they could see him salaam courteously on all sides, place his hand on his heart, his head; in fact, do everything short of kneeling or lying down which he could remember to have seen in the strange places of the Earth where his life had been chiefly spent.

Three of the curiously dressed figures who had been working the telescope, or gun, or electric machine, or whatever the curious instrument may have been, gathered round him, and it was evident the bold explorer had made a favourable impression. He bowed and scraped and waved his hand aloft, and then towards the mechanical contrivance with obvious meaning. It appeared as if he had been understood, for one of the men—I may call them men at once, for they were almost identical in physical organisation to human beings, with only some characteristic differences, of which more anon —one of the men went to the machine and moved it slightly out of line with the air-ship, which immediately commenced to fall at the same rate as before its progress had been arrested.

When the Steel Globe reached the ground the rope ladder was lowered, and the party scrambled down the side. MacGregor introduced them in dumb show to an elderly Mars man, behind whom a younger man and a boy ranged themselves. The terrestrials bowed low and the celestials copied their movements exactly. It was

evident that the latter courteously wished to set their
visitors at ease, but were not accustomed to the gesture,
for the boy smiled covertly as he bent his head.

Barnett advanced to the venerable host, and drawing
from his pocket a chart of the solar system on which he
had traced the journey from the Earth by a red line,
placed the paper in the hands of the Martian gentleman.
He had also a rough map of Mars, and on this he pencilled his course southwards from the spot in the Secchi
continent where they had landed. This he also handed
to the Martian professor, and by a sign suggested a
simultaneous examination of both. The parchments
were accepted with courteous, if slightly awkward, bows,
and compared with evident interest. The Martian beckoned his youthful companions to his side, and explained
the position of affairs, which, it afterwards transpired, he
had comprehended at a glance. Meanwhile, the men
from the Earth stood still and waited. While they wait I
may refer to their new acquaintances.

In stature the Martians were smaller than a man of
medium height, but their figures were so admirably pro-
portioned that this was not apparent unless an actual
comparison was made by placing a man close beside one
of them. Their heads were larger than what we would
consider to be in keeping with perfect symmetry, but
their bearing was so graceful no ungainly effect was
observable. The only very striking characteristic which

they possessed was the expression of their faces. One look at a Martian's face would convince the most obstinate sceptic that in them the *animal* had been suppressed and supplanted by the *intellect*. It is not always thus with us.

As to costume, our funereal clothing, or anything like it, was not known amongst them. They dressed. They did not merely cover their bodies. In colour, material, and make, they chose their garments so as to adorn themselves as well as protect themselves—not disguise, distort, burlesque themselves. In this matter, however, it must in fairness be admitted, they had one supreme advantage over us. Most of us have very little time to think how we are dressed. Most of these Martians had very little else to do but dress themselves. Their flowing robes of green and gold and grey would tarnish quickly in our work-a-day world. Their bright-hued tunics and brilliant sashes and tinted hose would be woefully out of place in a London fog. Fortunately for them, they had practically no work-a-day world, and absolutely no London fogs.

It will be more convenient if I begin at the beginning by calling these Martian people by their names : that is, by the names they were eventually known by amongst MacGregor's command. These names were in few cases either literally or even approximately correct. Sometimes they were a free translation ; sometimes an attempt at the sound of the Martian name; and sometimes a corruption of both. Thus, the Professor whom we left explaining the rude charts to his son and intended son-in-law, they called Dr. Profundis, partly because his own name sounded like that word, and partly because Blake thought it an excellent title for so learned a man. The " Dr." was an after-thought. There were no titles in Mars. Then the Professor's daughter, Mignonette, whom we shall meet later, was so called because her name was after that of a pretty little Martian flower closely resembling in blossom and perfume our own sweet plant. Many other names were given in this way to the numerous persons whom the adventurers encountered during their stay on the planet. Further explanation might prove tedious. Let us pass on.

When Dr. Profundis had explained the charts to his young people he went to a receptacle near the machine, which had given such sudden pause to Barnett's ship and drew forth a very large and magnificently executed astronomical chart. Turning to Barnett, he pointed out the Earth on this map. Barnett bowed assent. Then he waved his hand around and pointed to Mars on the chart. Barnett again made a gesture of assent. Exclamations of pleased astonishment escaped from the younger Martians. The Professor had succeeded in dispelling their doubts. They were overwhelmed with wonder and watched Barnett and his friends with close attention.

From the same receptacle Dr. Profundis now brought another and larger chart. This was too much for Barnett. Beautifully as it was drawn, its wealth of detail made it unintelligible to the scientist, wide as was his own knowledge. He handed it back to the Professor with a sense of humiliation he had never known before. But what could a man make of a chart of the solar system in which not merely hundreds, but actually thousands of Asteroids were as carefully mapped, the inclination of their orbits as accurately given, the periods of their revolution as minutely calculated, and their size and volume as exactly defined as we could deal with Jupiter the giant. It took Barnett a long time to master that map—but he did it at last.

Dr. Profundis was now puzzled. He knew where his visitors came from, and had also the knowledge that they had come of a set purpose. How to treat them, now that they had arrived, seemed a difficult question. He thought for a moment, and then, beckoning his visitors to follow him, he led the way to his house. The youth and the lad bowed and smiled reassuringly, at the same time pointing to the Steel Globe, as much as to say that they would keep a careful watch over it during the absence of its owners. The latter, therefore, followed the Professor without apprehension.

The entrance-door to the Professor's villa—palace, it might well be called—opened off a balcony of variegated marble. But this lofty promenade was fully twenty feet from the ground, and there was neither staircase to it nor any visible means of ascent.

"How is he going to climb it, Barnett?" MacGregor asked. "I suppose they manage everything with lifts. Too lazy to walk upstairs!"

"I think not," Barnett answered slowly.

"I shouldn't wonder if he 'swarmed up' the pillars," Sir George Sterling remarked. "I could climb a pole myself in this glorious planet." Sir George was overjoyed to find that he had walked up a slight incline without losing breath. He forgot that his sixteen stone of solid flesh on Earth weighed little over six on Mars, owing to the diminished attraction of gravitation on the latter planet. No wonder he felt his youthful energy returning!

"By Heaven, he can fly!" Blake exclaimed, clutching MacGregor's arm. Every man stopped. The Professor had, in fact, walked quietly up to his house, and then, without a moment's hesitation, or any apparent effort or preparation, he rose easily in the air, and stepped on the high balcony.

The party below stood still in amazement, and showed a line of perturbed faces. Dr. Profundis saw that something was wrong. He stood on the edge of the balcony twenty feet above their heads. Without the least show of hesitancy he stepped off.

"Get out of the way," MacGregor cried, forgetting that it must be as easy for the Professor to step down as to step up.

Advancing to Barnett, whom he rightly regarded as the most highly educated man of the party, the Professor offered his hand. Barnett accepted it at once. Immediately both were standing on the balcony above.

"I say, MacGregor, you go next," Blake urged, shoving the explorer forward. "You are—are better used to this sort of motion. That drop of yours was a great experience."

"Certainly," MacGregor assented. By this time the Professor had dropped down for another instalment. Without the least fatigue he repeated the movement, giving his hand to every man in turn till all were up. Then he opened a massive marble door balanced so exquisitely that it yielded to the slightest finger push, and by a polite gesture invited his guests to enter his house.

The main hall into which the party were ushered was very large. It was more like a place for public assembly than an apartment in a private gentleman's mansion. The lofty ceiling was exquisitely painted in imitation of the sky at mid-day. Pillars of polished marble—manufactured marble—supported the roof. Choice plants grew to almost tree-like luxuriance. Pretty little singing birds flitted in and out through open lattices, perching now on the fairy-like branches of a hot-house shrub, then

chattering gaily forth to rest on the murmuring boughs
of a garden plant without. There were no fires, no
apparent means of lighting the room at night, no footmen
in plush and powder; and yet the air within was warm
and pleasant, the hall could be gaily illuminated at a
moment's notice, and every office that the best trained
servant could render was diligently performed. Turn a
handle and a sultry heat, or polar frost, or any desired
degree of heat or cold between the two obtained. When
the sun was set and darkness deepened, press a knob, and
the vaulted roof flashed into the glory of a midnight sky
besprinkled with a thousand stars, every star a brilliant
point of vivid light, and two bright incandescent circles
representing the twin moons of Mars. Place your superfluous garments on a stand, and straightway they and it
disappeared in the most puzzling fashion.

"It is too bad, Graves," Blake grumbled. "I put
my umbrella down on a machine at the door and the whole
business has vanished. I suppose they have shot it into
the Sun, as Barnet feared they would MacGregor. I paid
sixteen-and-sixpence for it, too."

"For the machine?"

"For the machine! For the umbrella. You would
not joke about it if it was your own case."

"Wouldn't I? I have lost my overcoat."

"That's some satisfaction. Then you are as badly off
as I am."

"Worse.   I have lost my pipe."

Blake could not ignore the magnitude of this loss to Graves; so he said no more about his umbrella.

The Professor consulted a tablet, which was covered over with figures as manifold and puzzling as a railway guide, and then led the way to a special wing of the mansion.   The corridors were richly draped.   Beautiful pictures adorned the walls.   Rich draperies overhung the doorways.   Deep carpeting muffled every footfall.   It was not a house.   It was an enchanted castle—an actuality, the like of which on earth only exists in the creations of our imaginative writers.   But imagination is akin to prophecy.

The long corridors were unpeopled.   The rooms were empty.   The ladies of the household were from home, and Dr. Profundis was living for the time being alone with his son.   There was, therefore, no difficulty in providing rooms for the "surprise party," which had arrived. MacGregor and Barnett were sadly in need of rest.   The others had had some hours of restless sleep, but they were not sorry to hear from Barnett that their host did not expect them before dinner.   This intelligence was conveyed by a simple code of signals which was rapidly developing between the Martian professor and Mr. Barnett.

There was nothing very singular about the bedrooms unless it were the extreme simplicity, and at the same time exquisite taste, in which they were furnished. Colours which have a restful influence on weary eyes were predominant. The bathroom attached to each was a realistic imitation of a sea-drenched cavern. The action of stepping into bed caused a soothing strain of low music to whisper a gentle lullaby round the balmy pillow. In twenty minutes every man was sound asleep.

For fully ten hours they rested and renewed their strength. Then they were awakened by electric bells, and arose refreshed—new men, in fact. It was night without, but within, the mansion was as bright as noon. From unseen sources a hundred tinted lights filled every room and corridor. The great hall was a blaze of mellow radiance. The mimic moons and stars shone brightly. A banquet was spread in the centre of the room.

In appearance and arrangement it was perfect. The serving of it was admirable, if somewhat startling. But the dishes were disappointing. They were too simple in ingredients and seasoning. The wines were weak. Conversation was, under the circumstances, very limited.

After each course the table and all that was upon it disappeared mysteriously. A fresh laid board supplied its place. There were no waiters (beneficent mortals !). Every necessary service was rendered by automatic mechanism, and well rendered. Yet the polite attentions of a machine instead of a man had a chilling effect on those who were not accustomed to the arrangement.

No doubt, the method has its own advantages—for instance, when the time for hats and great-coats arrives a certain economic superiority attaches to it.  But it was all so new to MacGregor and his party, that they were rather puzzled by it.

Then, again, although the banquet was so admirably served, and, although everything that a courteous, if silent, host could do to make it pass off agreeably was done, it was only a meal—it was not a feast.  Sir George Sterling did not wish to be too critical, but he was forced to admit that it fell short of his expectations.  It was evident that on Mars eating had degenerated into a mere incidental function, and had ceased to be the supreme object of life, as any good alderman of London knows it ought to be.

So apparent, however, had been the anxiety of the Professor for the welfare of his guests through all that silent entertainment, no man felt at liberty to enliven his corner of the table by even the simplest " aside."  It was, therefore, a relief when the last table and all its appurtenances disappeared whence it came, and Dr. Profundis beckoned his guests around him.  His object was soon apparent.  He was anxious to establish some systematic means of interchanging ideas.  This was not very difficult.  Master Profundis, young as he was, far excelled Graves in the use of his pencil.  He could sketch the most unfamiliar object with the speed and accuracy of a

public exhibitor, whose sheets are prepared beforehand.
But, although slower and, as could be plainly seen by
comparison of their respective methods, about a thousand
years behind the style of the young Martian artist,
Graves was indispensable to the pictorial conversation
which flowed pleasantly enough for some hours. The
Martians did not depend on mere articulate sounds to
convey their ideas. Facial expression, intonation, and
gesture, were all so largely—as they were habitually—
employed by them not merely as aids but as factors in
conversation, it was wonderful how quickly the two
parties progressed in mutual knowledge. This knowledge
was limited, of course, to elementary facts and incidents,
connected with the Earth and Mars, and the people by
whom these planets were inhabited, but it sufficed to
prepare our adventurers in some slight degree for the
wonderland through which they were to pass before many
days.

A certain curiosity was rising in the mind of all the
visitors. Had the Professor no womankind in his
family ? This curiosity was fittingly voiced by Blake,
who was possessed of much personal initiative in such
matters.

"Now, Graves," he whispered, "when you have done
so well, draw Durand and his sweetheart—his last one, I
mean—and show it to the Professor. He'll know what we
want. We want to see the ladies of the family, don't we?"

"We do," said all but Durand, who resented Blake's raillery.

"Then let Graves draw Durand and a girl—any girl—and we'll do the gesticulation."

Graves seized the idea and very soon sketched the required figures. The sketch was presented to Dr. Profundis, who smiled intelligently and handed it to his son, over whose bright young face a look of similar intelligence passed, and the same exclamation escaped from both:

"Ah, Mignonette!"

The master of the house hastened good-naturedly to comply with the request of his guests. He led the way to another large and magnificently furnished saloon. This was seated to accommodate about forty or fifty persons. The seats were ranged in tiers rising one above the other as in a theatre. But where the stage ought to have been there was only a blank wall, fitted with a great array of small discs. Beside every one of these discs a tube projected. Above the series there was a very curious mechanical contrivance unlike anything even the scientific Barnett had ever previously seen. Its use was soon explained.

By touching a spring, Dr. Profundis lowered the brilliant light which filled the room till it faded into a soft and shadowy twilight. Then he went close to one of the discs and spoke some words against it. Turning to his guests he raised his hand to enjoin attention. They waited silently, never doubting but some new marvel was in store for them.

Very softly at first, but gathering strength in a moment, a flow of sweet sound broke the silence. Faint indeed were the silvery accents, but audible distinctly and musical as the sighing of the summer wind. It was a voice at once serious, and yet, withal, glad. A still, small voice that fell on the stirred imagination of the soul-rapt listeners from earth and filled them with a strange new sense of human holiness.

Lower still the twilight dimmed, and there before their startled eyes stole the vision of a young girl enshrined in a strange halo of unfamiliar light. She was clothed in floating draperies—filmy—illusive—intangible—an iridescent cloud through which could be traced the outlines of her faultless form. Her hair was of the tint of ruddy gold that caught the soft light and framed her face in a saint-like aureole. Her eyes were violet-blue, spirituelle and fathomless—a sweet, bright face, and thoughtful—a face of exquisite loveliness, undimmed by a shadow of that soft melancholy which clings to everything of perfect beauty upon the earth.

On her appearance the music of her voice did not cease, nor was the spell which it had woven round the wonder-stricken listeners broken. They watched her with reverent awe, and gazed upon her face as they would upon the face of an angel.

Again the Professor pronounced the sweet name, "Mignonette!"

He smiled on the shadowy form with great tenderness and straightway with an answering smile and a gesture of infinite affection and love, and half regret, the vision passed away.

Then the master of the house came to Henry Barnett and placed a map before him. An explanation of the curious phenomenon was made chiefly by signs, assisted by a few simple words which the Professor had already learned. Barnett comprehended him quickly and turned to his comrades.

"The girl is his daughter," he said. "She is at the present moment on a visit to an island in the Kaiser sea, about six thousand miles away. He has asked her to return. She will be here to-morrow."

# CHAPTER XI.

## MIGNONETTE.

WALTER DURAND found little rest that night. His apartment, as we know, was charming. His couch was luxurious. But he could not sleep. At last he had discovered a theme worthy of his pen. His quick imagination wove restlessly all manner of magical dramas. His busy brain wrestled with marvellous plots. He was already in love with his subject. And what a subject!

He arose late. The mellow sun of Mars was high over the undulating Lagrange hills. The delightful dryness of the air was invigorating. Quaint, gaudy birds sang joyously in the pleasant groves around the Professor's mansion. Within the house sounds of music and conversation could be heard in a faint hum. And at last a peal of delicious, rippling laughter floated up from the balcony below his windows.

"It is Mignonette!" he cried, nervously, and finished his lazy toilet in hot haste. Then he muttered dismally, "Oh, these hideous clothes!" He looked at his figure in a mirror and groaned aloud.

" It is not a costume. It is a uniform fit only for a workhouse or a gaol. I wish I could borrow a suit from that young brother of hers—but it would not fit me, of course. How stupid of MacGregor not to think of—of these monstrous masquerading garments. I'll enter into an alliance with Graves. I know he thinks the costumes here splendid. I saw him sketching them last evening, every moment that they gave him peace."

Having finished dressing, Durand opened his window and looked down eagerly. He was disappointed. A boy —a mere male creature—was standing on the balcony and talking to Master Profundis, who was training some climbing plants to the pillars underneath.

" Another brother, I suppose," Durand said, contemptuously. " How like his voice is to Mignonette's. Ah, sweet Mignonette!" He was about to turn away from the window, but at that moment the lad on the balcony moved from his position, and then leaning over the balustrade, said some words to his brother below. Durand's attention became fixed. He found himself watching the movements of the youth and listening to the wonderful sweetness of his voice as he conversed.

" What delightful grace!" he reflected. " He poses like a gymnast. I wish Graves were here."

The lad was dressed in a costume somewhat different from anything Durand had yet seen. He wore a tight-fitting, pearl-grey tunic of some soft and glossy material not unlike our velvet. A smart little cap of the same material and colour fitted closely to his head. A sash of crimson and gold was fastened round his waist and tied in a large knot on the left side. Breeches cut to the shape of the limb were buttoned at the knee over stockings of very dark green, and these disappeared into dainty little silver-buckled shoes.

Graves's room was next to Durand's. In a moment the latter was knocking at the artist's door.

" Come out, Graves ! Quick, man !"

" What's the matter, Durand ?" Graves called carelessly back. " I am tired of novelties."

" Come out at once, or you'll regret it all your life," Durand exclaimed, at the same time rattling at the door as if he would break it in.

Graves opened the door and said: " Don't make such a row. What do you want ? "

" Look at that lad, Graves. There's suppleness of movement and grace of posture for you. Isn't he an Apollo with the waist of a girl and the grace of a Ganymede !"

Graves burst into a rhapsody of delight. The artist was entranced. His sparing use of language which was partly natural and partly affected gave place to a torrent of declamation. For the moment he was as fluent as Blake, as eloquent as Barnett.

" See, he is going away. Run down, Durand, and

keep him there till I get a couple of outlines blocked in. Don't let him go, if you have to hold him by force. And turn his face a little fuller. That profile is good, but I want to get more of his expression."

Durand hurried down and passed out on the balcony just as the boy was about to leave it, and drop to the ground in that curious, easy-going way the Martians had of getting up and down stairs.

" I beg your pardon, sir," Durand commenced, at the same time laying his hand on the boy's shoulder. He did not, of course, expect to be understood, but he hoped to create a diversion of which Graves could take advantage.

The boy turned with that easy grace of movement which had already fired the artistic soul of Graves.

" Good heaven!—I am extremely sorry—I beg your pardon—I had no idea it was—it was you," Durand stammered, this time wholly oblivious of linguistic obscurity. "Please forgive me, Miss—Miss Mignonette, I believe." Durand removed his hat and bowed low.

It was indeed Mignonette! But what masquerade was this? None whatever. It was simply Mignonette dressed in her aërial costume—Mignonette by daylight.

The women of Mars—as might be expected in so advanced a world—were accorded all the privileges of the men. Like them they were instructed, as a part of their education, in that strange exercise of what may be called—in default of a better name—animal electricism.

This discovery enabled the Martians to regulate at will the attraction of gravity upon them so that they could move at any distance they wished from the ground. The exercise of so important a function was too exhausting to be continued for any considerable time, but even its temporary employment was very convenient. It was thus a very common thing to see the Martian ladies drift through the air on business or pleasure bent—and it had been decided to modify their dress to suit this method of transit.

The girl looked at Durand with child-like wonder. Here was one of the strange beings from another world of whom she had heard—of whom all Mars had heard, though their arrival was only a thing of yesterday. But good news travels fast in Mars. There is never any ill news there.

Mignonette was quite self-possessed. Durand was quite the opposite. She saw that he was ill at ease, and she raised her slender white hand to her forehead with a puzzled air. She seemed trying to recollect some difficult lesson: difficult from its absolute novelty. Suddenly a look of satisfaction passed over her face. She advanced frankly to Durand, and in a pretty, pleased way offered her hand, at the same time saying, with bewitchingly awkward articulation, "Good morning."

"Good morning," Durand responded, still very confused. Then nothing more was said. Mignonette had got to the end of her earthly dialogue, and Durand knew not a word of Mars. MacGregor, Barnett, Sterling, and Gordon had all been presented to her already, and, as the simplest formula, they had all used those words. Having heard them repeated so often Mignonette ventured on their use, and succeeded as well as an average foreigner does with our difficult language.

An awkward pause ensued, in which Durand furtively regarded his newly made acquaintance. There was nothing furtive in the way Mignonette regarded him. Her candid curiosity had not a trace of rudeness in it. But it was very trying to Durand.

This silent *tête-à-tête* was interrupted by Blake, who appeared on the balcony, one would have thought at an opportune moment. And yet Durand thought his presence inopportune. Blake did not wait for an invitation. He immediately introduced himself. Mignonette offered her hand, and with a bright smile repeated her whole stock of English language, saying "Good morning," in the same delightfully quaint "foreign" accent.

Durand could have remained for a long time without weariness, satisfied to watch the ever-varying expression of the girl's face. Almost every thought that passed through her mind was reflected in her mobile features as in a mirror. Her power of facial expression exceeded that of the Martian persons whom Durand had already met—even that of Dr. Profundis himself. There was surprise, anxiety to please, hopeless efforts to construct some plan of making herself understood, and an amused appreciation of the curious situation, all plainly to be read in the girl's bright young face.

"If you want any breakfast, Durand, you had better go in. I came out to look for you."

"You are much too kind, Blake—very much."

"Not at all, my dear fellow. It's only a pleasure to look after you—one is always sure of something worth seeing," Blake added meaningly, but with perfect good humour.

"In future perhaps you would be content to look after yourself," Durand began rather angrily, but Blake persisted with irritating amiability:

"After you—if you don't mind. You spy out the land so admirably. Do have some breakfast."

"I—I don't want any breakfast. I—did not sleep well last night. I have no appetite."

"Nonsense! you never looked better. Hurry in and get something to eat. I'll keep Miss Mignonette amused for you till you come back."

That settled it. Durand turned away, wondering how it came about that he had never before noticed what a meddlesome, ill-mannered and generally objectionable man Blake was.

"Now that's sensible," Blake called after his retiring companion. "Make a good meal, Durand. You need not hurry back, you know." There was a twinkle in the Irishman's mirthful blue eyes as he fired this final shot after the vanquished Durand.

"Thank you," Durand was understood to answer, as he entered the house, but the remark did not sound quite like that to MacGregor, who met him in the doorway.

"Where have you been, Durand ? We were beginning to fear you were ill, and were just about to bring the medicine chest up to you."

"I declare you have all become extremely careful about me. I have been standing on the balcony for two minutes. Blake rushes out, hysterical about my breakfast. You threaten your medicine chest. Has Gordon or Sir George anything to add ?"

"Why, what is this, Durand ? What have I said to annoy you ?" MacGregor said uneasily. "You're not usually so easily vexed."

"I am not vexed, but I wish you wouldn't all make such a fuss about nothing."

"Well, well, don't think any more about it. No offence taken where none is meant, I hope. Where is Graves ? "

"He is sketching from the window of his room."

"Then we shan't see him to-day if he has settled down to that."

"He will be down presently. He won't sketch long."

"It's the first time I ever knew him to drop it so easily. Perhaps it's the climate. What is he sketching ?"

"Miss—Mignonette."

"Miss Mignonette! where is she?"

"She is—on the balcony."

"Ah, I understand." There was a good deal of meaning in MacGregor's exclamation. "And who is with her now?"

"Blake and be——" Durand stopped short.

"Humph!" MacGregor looked wise. "Well, go and have some breakfast, Durand"—at this moment Sir George Sterling and Gordon came out from the breakfast-room—"and while you are enjoying your food the rest of us will have a look at Miss Mignonette."

"Miss Mignonette!" said Sir George; "where is she?"

"On the balcony. Come this way. Have you got your note-book, Gordon? Now you will have something pretty to make a memorandum about."

"Of course I have," Gordon answered eagerly as he drew out his note-book. "Where is she?"

"This way, this way," MacGregor directed, leading them to the balcony where Blake and Mignonette were standing.

Durand was left alone. He made his way into the breakfast-room, muttering as he went, "Graves is sketching her, Blake is talking to her, or trying to talk to her, Gordon is—making memorandums about her, and the other two—the old fools—they are looking at her. Enjoy my food! Pah!"

# CHAPTER XII.

## THE OLD STORY.

DURAND found the breakfast-room empty. Barnett had been long since carried off by the Professor. These two were now hard at work in the library. They had much to learn from each other. Master Profundis was still in the garden. The Martian food which was on the table in abundance was not to Durand's taste. The remains of preserved meats, fruit, and fish taken from supplies of the Steel Globe, in pursuance of Sir George's instructions, were not appetising. But he preferred to breakfast off a few scraps rather than call into use those weird automatic arms which fetched and carried so admirably, but whose mechanism he feared to tamper with. It was not an excellent meal at best. It was rendered wretched by the sounds of laughter and broken sentences which floated in from the balcony. Mignonette was holding a reception and evidently enjoyed the fun of receiving strangers with whom she could only communicate by signs—and those wonderfully expressive features of hers.

The laughter outside ceased suddenly. Durand had

chafed at it while he listened to it. Now that it was gone, the silence was intolerable. He left the room and ran to the balcony. It was deserted. His friends were gone. That did not matter. Mignonette was gone—that did. There was only Mignonette's brother left. He was evidently waiting for the solitary guest who must not be left utterly alone, notwithstanding his reprehensible want of punctuality. Of course there was not much companionship in the presence of a boy with whom one could not exchange a word. Still his company was better than none. Besides, he resembled Mignonette very much.

Master Profundis came up to Durand, smiling in a friendly way. His play of feature, though less subtle than that of his sister, was considerable. He offered his hand to Durand, who accepted it with a bow, and immediately felt his own weight disappear. The sensation was exactly similar to that which he had experienced on the previous day when the Professor had floated him up. Both stepped off the balcony and sailed pleasantly to the ground. The Martian youngster then led the way to a pretty grove near the house, and here Durand found all his friends.

It was a strange and brilliant scene. The sunlight passed with a mellow richness through overhanging and luxuriant foliage. Bright flowers burned sweet incense to the god of day. Fountains plashed harmoniously in marble basins. Music from an unseen source trembled in the air. Pretty, fawn-like animals wandered fearlessly

about, nibbling at a stray shoot of vegetation or pressing
their pretty heads caressingly against their loving captors'
hands.   Bright feathered birds sat undismayed on every
bending branch, and billed and cooed, and sang sweet
carols rich with the fresh melody of woodland joy.  Butter-
flies with downy wings of rainbow hues flitted hither and
thither.   And brighter still than they were the kaleido-
scopic but restful colours of the wondrous costumes of
the throng of Martian visitors now assembled—deep, rich
colours for the men, soft, soothing tones for the matrons,
delicate tints for the maidens, bright and sparkling hues
for the youths.  It was a morning reception.  The crowded
attendance was due to the general curiosity awakened by
the presence of the men from another world.   Old age
was here without ugliness, maturity without boastfulness,
youth without tawdry conceit.  And all ages and both sexes
bore themselves with the same calm politeness, the same
absolute respect.

   MacGregor, the great explorer, lay back in a luxurious
lounge with an air of long-forgotten quiescence.   The
baronet sprawled flat on the velvet turf and thought no
more of finance.   Graves seemed hardly conscious of the
lovely lights and shadows, and Gordon took no notes.
Blake, indeed, was more like his old self.   Mignonette
was there.   She was sitting at one end of a low couch.
Another girl, her special friend, sat at the other; and
Blake sat between.   These Irish have few supreme

characteristics. They are tenacious of the few they have.

As for Durand, after his first introduction to the Professor's guests, he stood aside and sulked. Now a strange thing would have struck this knight of the pen had he been in his ordinary mind : that is, the mind of a literary man who sees everything, observes everything, weighs everything, studies it, calculates it, asks its why and wherefore, racks his brain over it, who is an inventor of situations, an anatomist of characteristics, a scientist of trivialities, and the strange thing was this :—Dr. Profundis in an evening and a morning had mastered a fairly complete knowledge of the rudiments of the English language. This knowledge was complete enough to enable him to give his family and his friends some slight account of the strange visitors from the Earth.· It was exact enough to enable him to translate the remarks, questions, and comments of Barnett, who sat near him, and who, subdued by the languorous delight of beatific surroundings, wondered lazily at the inexplicable intellect with which he was now confronted. This marvellous intellectual power surpassed in grasp and brilliancy anything that the man of earthly science could ever before have dreamed of. Even sweet Mignonette had progressed, under Blake's tuition, from her pretty little hesitating " Good morning," and was now able to say a few simple sentences very correctly, and to understand their meaning.

But neither Blake nor·Barnett had so far learned one
Martian word.   The reason of this is easily understood.
The intellects on one side had the start of the intellects
on the other by many thousand years.

So they all sat under the soft foliage of the delicate
trees and listened to the music sighing in a soft accom-
paniment to the pleasant monotone of the morning breeze.
And through the medium of Barnett and the Professor
they chatted in simple but sincere words with those courteous Martians, to whom they told the wonderful story of
their journey from the Earth.   Who shall blame them if
for a few brief moments, after all the mad excitement of
their grand enterprise, they forgot the pith and moment
of their task, forgot, perhaps, in that land of luxury and
love that there existed a far-away, half barbaric, wholly
restless and sorrowful earth, a weary and heavy-laden earth
in the scheme of that· creation whose dreadful mysteries
they themselves had been the first mortal men to dare.

Never did time gallop more madly with love-lorn swain
and love-charmed maid than he did through that short
sixty minutes of perfect rest.   But then he sharpened
his ruthless scythe and swore that another hour had been
cut down like the grass that withereth.   Then those
courteous Martians gathered round them their cloaks of
green and gold and grey and purple, and made their farewells.   The Professor conveyed to Barnett that he and his
companions were expected to amuse themselves for an

hour or two. The short working day of Mars—about two hours—had begun, and all had duties to which they must attend.

So the happy Martians flitted off; some walking decently and in order by the flower-bordered pathways; some flitting bird-like over the tree-tops. Presently all were gone, and only the adventurers remained to bear each other company. It was then that Durand, who still stood sullenly apart from his friends, felt a light touch upon his arm. It was Mignonette. She had returned for a moment, proud of the pleasure she felt sure it was in her power to convey. Her great soft eyes were full of gladness. She smiled with a witchery that would have charmed a heart of stone. There was a world of sympathy in her sweet face. Durand felt his blood tingle. She had singled him out. She was weary of Blake. She had come to him to whisper some simple sentence to comfort him in his lonely and neglected misery.

She had indeed learned a simple sentence and learned it, too, for his especial benefit. But her English education was still sadly deficient, for, with a pretty smile and just a touch of gentle camaraderie, she said in that curious foreign accent of hers:

" It is a fine day."

Durand actually scowled on her, and poor, kind-hearted Mignonette turned away with two great tears, almost the first she had ever shed, trembling in her long lashes.

"That unfeeling scamp, Blake," Durand raged, "he did it purposely. I'll swear he did—oh, Mignonette, I did not mean—" but Mignonette had disappeared, and only the memory of a sorrowful sigh was left to him.

"Well, Durand, day-dreaming as usual!" Blake said in his off-hand way, at the same time thrusting his arm through his friend's. "Come and take a stroll through the grounds while I tell you all about Miss Mignonette."

"I don't want to hear anything about Miss Mignonette," Durand replied, wrenching his arm free. "I really do wish, though, that you would be sensible, Blake. You are becoming very tiresome about this girl."

"I never knew you to be so easily tired about a nice girl before—and she is a nice girl, no matter what you may say."

"I never said she wasn't."

"You never said she was."

"Well then she is; and I think you are very ungentlemanly to speak of her as you do."

"Good Lord! Durand, what are you talking about. How am I to please you? If I say she is a nice girl you fly at me. If I speak of her at all I am ungentlemanly!"

"Then don't speak of her at all."

"Indeed! why not?"

"Because—oh, say what you like. I don't mind in the least."

"You're in an amiable mood this morning, Durand, but no matter. Perhaps your breakfast was not to your liking, so I must forgive you. To resume what I was about to say when you so rudely interrupted me, I have found out something about these Mars girls."

" Something very profound, I have no doubt."

" Well, it is not very profound ; but I dare say it is quite as accurate as anything Barnett has discovered, notwithstanding his long consultations with old De Profundis or whatever you call him."

" Professor Profundis," Durand corrected with marked coldness of manner.

" Professor Profundis by all means; but to return to the ladies, I was much struck with one curious point in which they differ from our own girls."

" Indeed ! what struck you particularly ?"

" Particularly and unpleasantly I was struck with the fact that they have lost the instinct of flirtation."

" It strikes me particularly and unpleasantly," Durand said in his grand manner, " that it is an instinct our girls could very well dispense with."

" And it also strikes me," Blake answered in his practical way, " that such a dispensation would leave them devilish dull company."

" In the present instance, as your ambition rose no higher than to teach—Miss Mignonette—to say it was ' a fine day,' perhaps you are rather premature in your judgment."

" Pshaw ! It isn't necessary to talk to a woman to

flirt with her. You take everything too seriously. You
don't understand how to pretend——"

"You should make allowances for those who are not
clever at pretence. We have not all had the advantage
of a political training."

Now this was a cruel thrust to Blake. In every
relation of life save one he was absolutely "straight."
But it must be admitted that in politics he would lie like
an ex-cabinet minister. He turned fiercely to Durand
and said :

"There are other and better schools for pretence than
politics. I would rather romance for a cause than
romance for a calling."

"Rubbish. You flirt with every woman you meet,"
Durand answered with equal bitterness.

"And you! You make love to them, all and sundry.
It seems we are quits."

"Then it is time we were quits in everything," Durand
said, and turned on his heel.

Blake muttered angrily under his breath, and walked
as resolutely in the opposite direction.

So they parted in anger. They had been fellow voyagers for fifty millions of miles, and in that strange
voyage they had singled out each other for special
friendship. It is only fair to remember, however, that
there was no woman in the Steel Globe by which they
had travelled so harmoniously.

# CHAPTER XIII.

## A MARTIAN DRAMA.

DR. PROFUNDIS thought it better to keep his guests in his house that evening. They were so new to the ways of the Martian world he decided to give them a week's rest before venturing to take them abroad. This delay was irksome to some of the visitors, although there were ample resources for their edification in the Professor's mansion. They were eager to see the wonders of the inhabited countries of Mars, but their thoughtful host wisely restrained them. He was anxious that they should be accustomed gradually to their new surroundings, lest they should act unwisely. He was right in this, for, notwithstanding his precaution, some of them acted foolishly the moment a suitable opportunity arrived.

Madame Profundis, a magnificent matron, was present at dinner. She had returned with her daughter by the night express from that island in the Kaiser sea, six thousand miles away. This distance was easily covered in a single night by the aërial ship in which they travelled. The ladies wore the filmy, floating draperies which constituted the evening dress of Martian women. Mignonette, indeed, was dressed in the same costume she had worn when her counterfeit presentment appeared on the previous evening. With the pleasant exception of the ladies' society, the dinner was very like its predecessor. There was the same absence of waiters, the same light food, and the same weak wines. There was, however, a little more conversation, for during the day great progress had been made by the Martians in the leading language of the Earth.

As soon as dinner was over, the Professor led the way to the saloon, where the vision of Mignonette had appeared. It was brilliantly lighted, and the seats were arranged as if in expectation of company. This expectation was quickly fulfilled. Many of the people who had been present at the garden party of the morning came in, and with them, others, whose faces were new. The truth was, the news of the Professor's guests had spread far and wide, and intense interest was taken in them. People who had not visited Dr. Profundis for months came trooping in, eager to see the adventurous strangers, and hear all that could be told of them. No disagreeable curiosity was manifested, but Mignonette had a busy time with her girl friends.

"What are they doing now, MacGregor?" Blake asked. Signs of hesitation were apparent, both on the part of the Professor and his Martian guests.

"Ask Barnett; I can't make the old gentleman understand anything I say."

Barnett was requisitioned immediately. The Professor saw that his presence was desired, and came over to them at once. After a few disjointed sentences and a vast expenditure of gesture, Barnett said:

"They are discussing what form of entertainment would be most likely to please us, and are at a loss how to decide."

"Why don't they vote?" Blake said, promptly.

This suggestion was duly conveyed to the Professor, and its meaning explained. He seized the idea readily, and informed his company, who, with much amusement, proceeded to carry out the proposal. This method of settling a difference of opinion was quite new to them. The foolish Martians did not actually know that the majority are invariably right, that their judgment is always the wisest, their decision always the best. But the good humour of the Martians was undeniable, if their methods were crude. The question was decided by a show of hands—a ceremony presided over by Blake, with Barnett as an interpreter.

"The ayes have it," the politician pompously announced, with a slight mixing of methods.

"Have what?" Gordon asked excitedly, note-book in hand. "How did the division go? What was it about?"

"You had better ask Barnett," Blake answered, contentedly resuming his seat. He had done his part.

Again the simple Martians laughed pleasantly. Not even a show of hands seemed to impress them. But they courteously agreed that the question should be determined after the strange fashion of the Earth.

The choice had lain between a scientific lecture with diagrams, and a very old drama of early Lagrange life, which had lately been revived on account of its historical interest, and with great success. Anything possessed of historic interest was very popular in Mars. So the play was produced.

"I should have liked to see the diagrams," Barnett plaintively observed. But no one heeded him.

"It is all very well to decide on a play, but who is to act?" Gordon asked. He was eager to write his first dramatic criticism on the Martian drama.

"It does not matter about the acting," Graves said; "we shall have a sight of some rare old costumes," and he prepared to sketch.

"Yes," said Blake, "according to Barnett's theory this play should bring us back to tall hats and trousers. Perhaps the date is prior even to our period, and we shall have something Shakespearean. I should not mind playing Orlando, with Miss Mignonette as Rosalind."

"You would do better as Touchstone," Durand growled.

MacGregor and Sir George prepared to sleep. The

play was not much in their way. Barnett's mind was soon lost in the mazy multitudes of the Milky Way.

Dr. Profundis seated himself amongst the strangers from the Earth. He hoped to help them to an appreciation of the various scenes about to be acted. The ladies occupied the front seats and did not wear high hats. So far, there was no more appearance of a stage than there was of actors. There was, however, a stage bell. It rang musically. The Professor lowered the rich light. The gorgeous hangings waved their shadowy folds in a dim soft gloom.

"It will be the Mignonette vision trick over again," Blake whispered.

Durand heard him and his eyes blazed angrily at the flippant comment.

At that moment the end of the room burst into a blaze of light. A stage as large and as luxuriously festooned with foliage as the gardens around the Professor's mansion magically appeared. A burst of music rang out clamorously. Then a great company of actors took up the complicated story and set it forth with so much grace of gesture, so much expression of countenance and such admirable and artistic stage grouping, that even those who did not know the meaning of a spoken word could follow minutely the development of the plot, and mark the progress of the play.

And such a play! A drama of the combatant age

written by a scientific dramatist, and played by Millennial
actors! What gentle oppressors! what chivalrous con-
querors! what tender tyrants! what humanitarian
murderers, thieves and rascals! As well might the slave
trade have been suppressed by a plentiful scattering of
tracts, or Waterloo have been won by a lady's school!

It delighted the Martian part of the audience however.
They had before them the picturesqueness of struggle
without its miseries, the romance of rescue without the
guilt of wreckers, the glory of victory without the horrors
of defeat. To the men fresh from the epoch which these
gentle players parodied so sweetly, the play, though meant
in solemn earnest, was a medley as grotesque as an opera
bouffe, as false and foolish as the wildest conglomerate of
Kingsley or Scott.

Gordon and Graves were busy. For them this was a
field laden with golden grain. Barnett was in the clouds.
MacGregor and the baronet slept peacefully after the first
act. Blake succeeded in establishing a mild flirtation
with a playful maid of Mars. But Durand was gloomy.
He pretended to be grateful for the Professor's polite
attentions but all the time he was furtively watching
Mignonette. She was surrounded by a bevy of spirituelle
girls, whose colour came and went according to the
fortunes of the impossible hero in the play. Only that
strong emotions were unknown in Mars they might even
have wept for him. For indeed he was as charming as

Sir Galahad ; the heroine was as pathetic as Elaine ; and both were likewise as unreal and untrue.

"What do you think of it, Graves?" Gordon asked when the curtain fell on the last act—that is to say, when the whole scene, actors, stage, theatre and all had melted away and left nothing but a dead wall in their place.

"Bosh !" the laconic Graves replied. His criticism, if inelegant, was accurate.

Afterwards there was a short sketch representing modern life in Mars, and in this a very faithful picture was given of the idyllic life in that happy planet. It was also a little monotonous—as perfection is apt to be. One of the actresses in this piece resembled Mignonette very closely in face, figure and voice. This gave the slight drama a personal interest to Durand and his friends it would not otherwise have possessed. They felt certain that the figure on the stage was really that of the Professor's daughter reproduced in some of the strange Martian methods.

Then there was music played by unseen hands, and one or two songs, the singers of which were seen as well as heard—seen in the same visionary unreality which had shrouded the first appearance of Mignonette as well as the actors in the plays.

Conversation followed, and everything thenceforth was arranged very like one of our evening parties. But there was no dancing, nor anything like it. When Dr. Profundis was questioned on this point he roundly declared that the Martians would no more have consented to whirl in the silly motion of the valse, or tread the solemn farce of the quadrille, than they would have betaken themselves to the woods, undressed and greased their bodies to circle with dreadful war-whoops and brandishings of hatchets round an iron pot supplied with meat of doubtful origin. The Professor's views were really very advanced.

When the company were about to break up they all pressed round the " foreigners," anxious to show them every possible mark of courtesy. " Good night, good night," sounded on every side. The thoughtful Martians had made up this short sweet greeting in order to give pleasure to the pilgrims from a distant planet. At last they were gone, and MacGregor, having said good-night to the Professor and his family, led his followers to the wing which had been set apart for their accommodation.

" Come to my room," he said, " we shall have a pipe before going to bed. I feel as if I had not smoked for six months." No one smoked on Mars. On receiving this invitation Graves brightened wonderfully.

" What is Barnett about ? " the baronet asked.

" Oh, don't mind him. He does not smoke ! Besides, he is going to sit up with the Professor."

" Is the Professor unwell ? "

" Nonsense, he wants to have a long talk with Barnett."

"They will be pleasant company with only half a dozen sentences of common ground between them."

"They will have more than that to-morrow."

"How?"

"Barnett is going to give him finishing lessons in the English language to-night. The whole family will know it in a week."

"They must be a smart family," Blake surmised. The breach between him and Durand was closing fast under the soothing influence of Sir George's grand cigars. His next remark opened it wide again and deep.

"What fun it will be, talking to that pretty chit, Mignonette!"

There was thunder in the air, but MacGregor, whose instinctive knowledge of men was very keen, interrupted with a shrug of comfort:

"I haven't felt as much at home since we left Alaska."

"We are pretty comfortable certainly, and now that we are here, MacGregor," Blake said, "tell us what we are to do in Mars and how we are to do it. You don't expect us to loiter about the Professor's garden all our time."

"I can tell you nothing yet. Barnett has only been able to get a vague idea as to the state of the country. I must say it is surprising how he has gathered what little he does know, and I must also admit that what he has learned is not very encouraging."

" Is it discouraging ? "

" Well, perhaps not so bad as that. The truth is, I am afraid it is only a dead-and-alive sort of place at the best."

" It seemed lively enough to-day, what with people flying about over the tops of trees, and Mignonette and her mother travelling home six thousand miles in a night."

" Ah, that reminds me. I have something interesting to tell you about that."

Anything about Mignonette must be interesting. Eager expectancy was on every face. Sir George even forgot for the moment how unsatisfactory his dinner had been.

" Yes," said MacGregor, " it's about that curious yell we heard in the Secchi continent."

" Damn the Secchi continent. We had enough of it —it's not a pleasant subject. Tell us about Mignonette," Blake interrupted.

MacGregor looked at him lazily through the blue smoke of his cigar.

" You seem to be in a hurry about Miss Mignonette."

" Well—the fact is—oh, go on with your story. We crossed the Secchi continent. Assume that much and let us hear the rest."

" Very well, I assume it. I also assume that you all remember a disagreeable howl."

" You are right, we are not likely to forget it."

" It was caused by the passage of an aërial car going at the rate of a thousand miles an hour. Mignonette travelled home in a similar car last night—fact ! "

" Good heavens ! "

A rain of questions followed, but MacGregor put up his hand deprecatingly.

" You need not ask me. It is not my line. Barnett will tell you all about it later."

" Very well, MacGregor; but surely you will tell us all you know about this wonderful world."

" What I know is, as I have told you, very little; but—" he stretched himself more comfortably, knocked a long white ash off the end of his cigar, and resumed— " here it is. It appears that they only work two hours a day, so there is no great hardship from overpressure. The population is stationary, or slightly decreasing, so there is no emigration. The whole planet is one nation, speaking one language, so they have no foreign complications. They are governed by one set of unchanging laws, so they have no politicians."

Here he looked hard at Blake, who tossed his head defiantly.

" Governed ! What then is their government like ? "

" There is no government worth speaking of," MacGregor answered.

Blake's countenance fell, but he professed indifference.

"What about their money market?" Sir George asked anxiously. "I hope they have a sound financial scheme."

"Well, as to a financial scheme," MacGregor answered carelessly, "I am not quite sure yet whether they have any scheme at all."

"What?" Sir George thundered.

"I said I did not know whether they used any form of money," MacGregor replied testily.

"Not—use—money! Ha! ha! ho! ho! very good, MacGregor, very good. Go on, go on." The baronet laughed satirically.

"It is very easy to say go on. I have told you all I know. I can go no farther."

"It isn't much," Graves commented. Then he removed his mighty pipe, and asked MacGregor in his pointed way: "What do you intend to do?"

"Barnett proposes to remain a year in Mars. That is equal to two of our years at home, or within a trifle of it—forty or fifty days I think."

"Forty-three days," Gordon read from his note-book.

"Well, I was pretty near it," MacGregor went on. "We are to occupy the time in 'doing' the planet. When the year is up the Earth will be in conjunction again, and we shall run across and tell our story."

"I like the expression 'run across,'" Graves observed.

"In the meantime," MacGregor continued, "every man

is bound by the unwritten articles he signed—to put it after the manner of our friend, Blake—to do his very best in his own especial groove for the general good. Durand and Graves will work up the literature and art of Mars. Blake and Sir George will have charge of its law and commerce. Gordon keeps an account of the journey. Barnett shall re-chart the heavens through these wonderful telescopes they have got here, and I shall run about and explore the place from pole to pole."

"Two years is a pretty long stay," several men said together.

"Too long for me," MacGregor admitted. "But you would not have us take a shot at the Earth when she is on the other side of the Sun, would you ?"

"I am afraid, MacGregor, we shall be all rather tired of this Utopian existence," Sir George said thoughtfully. "No money, indeed !"

"I daresay we shall," MacGregor replied. "I should not be surprised if there was not a nook or corner in the whole concern that was not explored centuries ago. I don't know how I shall get through the time—but it cannot be helped."

And Blake grumbled, "How is a man to make a telling speech in a language where the main element is grimace. If I can only get Miss Mignonette to teach me to make faces properly I'll—I'll show up the Government in a way that will astonish them."

Durand was silent. The two years did not seem an interminable period to him. He had Mignonette to " study."

When they had all retired MacGregor undressed languidly. Before he fell asleep he yawned drowsily, " I wonder—what—the planet—Jupiter—is like !"

# CHAPTER XIV.

### A CITY OF DELIGHT.

NEXT morning Durand was early astir. His prehistoric costume—as he called it—still gave him uneasiness, but it could not be helped; at least, not until he had seen a Martian tailor. He might as well have remained in bed. Mignonette did not appear. Instead of her, Blake came stealing out. The two men saluted each other shame-facedly, and each made an excuse as silly as the other to account for his presence on the balcony at such an early hour. One remembered that he had forgotten something, and the other forgot that he should have remembered something.

"I met young Profundis in there," Blake said with some constraint, but, at the same time, with an evident desire to allow the misunderstanding of the previous day to lapse.

"He is a very nice lad," Durand replied, trying to show some cordiality.

"He can talk English tolerably well now. He was up last night with Barnett and his father."

" Talk English ! Is it really possible ? Then Mac-Gregor was serious ! "

" Certainly ! The boy speaks as well now as an ordinary foreigner. By the way, he is to conduct us to the great city near this place. We start after breakfast. While we are away the Professor is to teach Mignonette as much as her brother knows.'

" So we are to see the city to-day. That will be very interesting. I thought we were to be kept here a week?"

" MacGregor got that arrangement changed this morning. He was up long ago, and worried Barnett into an appeal to the Professor to let us see the place to-day. Of course it will be interesting, but don't you think, Durand, you would prefer to remain and help to teach Miss Mignonette—I should."

" I wish to Heaven, Blake, you would give up dragging that girl's name into every conversation. It annoys me ; that's the candid truth."

" My dear fellow, I only did it to annoy you. That is also candid."

" And rather unkind—candour usually is."

" Perhaps it is, but you deserved it. You seemed to think you had a peasant proprietorship—oh, bother it, I mean a personal proprietorship over the girl. I did not see the justice of your claim. Therefore I disputed it."

" Nonsense, Blake, you were just as selfish as I could have been."

"I must have been tolerably bad then."

"Now listen to me, Blake. We are neither of us, I suppose, worse than the average, but, seriously, are we either of us worthy of——"

"No!" said Blake emphatically; "we're not!"

"Then let us be sensible and think no more about her. The girl is more like an angel than a woman.'

"I won't promise all that, but I am willing to stop chaffing you about her. Let us swear a mighty oath of joint allegiance to sweet Mignonette, and let the first article of our faith be, no flirtation on my part, no making of love on yours. Honestly speaking, it would be a shame."

"Agreed!" said Durand; and thus the friendship which the fascination of Mignonette's beauty and winning ways had interrupted was renewed by the refining influence of her radiant spirit.

Neither the Professor nor Barnett appeared at breakfast. Their late sitting had lasted far into the night, and they were in need of the rest which MacGregor's early visit had disturbed. The ladies of the house were also absent; but Master Profundis played the host with the easy dignity of a mature man of the world. There was no delay made over the meal. The men were too anxious to start for the city. They ate with the zeal of commercial travellers.

Yielding to urgent request, Master Profundis soon brought the party out to inspect his aërial yacht. The hull of this curious vessel had all the graceful lines of a racer of the Solent, but, of course, the absence of masts and snow-white sails robbed it of its picturesqueness. Its outward construction was, indeed, wholly moulded for use—not ornament. The bow ended in a sharp point. The hull tapered back until its greatest bulk was attained. From that portion it narrowed in again to a thin point as sharp as the bow. In fact, the bow and stern ends were identical. They were also interchangeable, each in turn becoming bow or stern, according to the direction of the vessel's course—one on the outward and the other on the homeward voyage. The vessel made only these two direct trips. She could not move a yard to one side or the other of her permanent course from the Professor's house to the central station in the city. We shall know the reason of this presently.

MacGregor was walking up and down with hasty strides. Every five minutes he asked impatiently : " What is keeping Barnett ? We shall lose the whole day standing here. I never knew him to be so late."

Here Barnett appeared, accompanied by Dr. Profundis. They were conversing freely in simple sentences. The Professor was evidently much pleased with his new accomplishment. He commended the party to the guidance of his son in terms that were almost facetious.

"Ask him to go slow, Barnett," MacGregor said when they had taken their places. " We should like to see the country. That is, if he can regulate his speed."

"He can go at any speed he wishes, from a mile an hour to a thousand."

"One mile an hour will do for me," Blake protested.

"We'll be in for a collision to a certainty if he gets racing with some other young Martian's yacht."

"A collision is impossible," Barnett took upon himself to explain. Master Profundis still had some difficulty in fully expressing himself in English. "Every aërial yacht runs only in a direct line from its positive to its negative station or the reverse. No other vessel is allowed to come within a hundred yards of this course. The same rule is applicable to the great trunk-routes traversed by the enormous air-ships, such as we heard crossing the Secchi continent. Every vessel, public or private, has its own course separated by a certain fixed minimum distance from all others. In every instance this legal minimum is more than ample, for no ship or yacht could deviate from its line a hair's breadth. Collisions in this planet are impossible."

"Except in the case of a derelict like ourselves when we were drifting about that desert," MacGregor added.

Barnett admitted that that was one of the worst perils of the whole voyage.

By this time they were moving slowly through the air. Master Profundis went to one of the side-windows and kissed his hand towards the house they now were leaving behind.

"Look there, Durand. There she is," Blake whispered.

A shimmer of crimson and gold shone against the snowy white of the sculptures on the balcony. The men raised their hats, and Mignonette, copying the gesture, waved her little pearl-grey cap. Then in an attitude full of that wonderful grace of hers, she leaned against a slender pillar and watched the yacht pass out of sight in the distance.

As soon as his home and Mignonette were out of sight, Master Profundis increased the speed of the yacht to forty miles an hour. At this rate the panorama beneath was easily observed. The country over which they flew was the richest portion of habitable Mars. Here was the England of the planet. Much of the peninsula of Lagrange lies between the degrees of South latitude corresponding to those of North latitude upon the Earth which enclose the British Isles. It is the seat of what slight government obtains in Mars. Its people are not, indeed, more highly civilised or more scientific than those of other lands in Mars, for all are nearly equally advanced —any inequality being rather individual than racial. But Lagrange holds a unique position in the planet. From it, in the old days, had gone forth to the ends of Mars those warriors whose prowess subdued all manner of barbaric hordes, the very existence of which is inimical to

progress. And when the soldiers of Lagrange had pur-
chased with their lives a highway for its thankless
colonists, missionaries, merchants and mechanics, from it,
too, had proceeded all those insidious influences whereby
the work of conquest is completed, and the ground is
cleared for more useful races. Its factories had sent out
improved arms with which the conquered tribes might the
more quickly destroy each other. In lieu of precious
stones its merchants bartered rude knives, scandalously
bad, but sufficient to cut an enemy's throat; or gave
shoddy goods in exchange for fertile lands. And, lastly,
its schools had shed abroad that faint glimmer of knowledge which is less serviceable always to the savage than
the terror-worship of his own false gods.

Thus Lagrange, the pioneer of Martian civilisation,
had inherited by right, the acknowledged position of
leader of its consolidated and enlightened people, now
that the duties of nationhood had passed away. This
precedence was of a purely academic nature. Lagrange
was, doubtless, the seat of government, the centre of
learning, the temple of art, the metropolis of commerce,
the hive of industry, in Mars. Yet all these were of a
nature peculiar to themselves—at least their functions
were unlike anything in our world. Employment, which,
in the severest occupations, only lasted two or three hours
a day, strikes our earthly understanding as more like the
amenities of a highly salaried Government appointment

than the duties of an industrial career.  Commerce, which
knew no vicissitudes of price, or crop,  or disaster at sea,
or foreign competition, hardly deserves comparison with
our own grand gamble, and all its wild chances, heroic
plungers,  brilliant  speculators,  princely fortunes,  and
ghastly failures.   Science, literature, and art, which consisted mainly in a contemplative study of past masters,
seems to our  minds as useless as a Government which is
rarely expected and  hardly ever called upon to govern ;
which never makes any new laws, and not once in a
hundred years administers its old ones ; which has neither
ships of war nor heavy guns ; no soldiers,  no sailors, no
police,  no gaols,  no judges,  no wicked lawyers—nor
even good lawyers, if indeed there be any such—and,
strangest fact of all,  a Government which collected no
taxes.

I have digressed.   These matters were not yet made
plain to MacGregor or his band.

As the aërial yacht moved gaily over the long sloping
landscape, which swept down from the mountain to the
golden shores of the Maraldi sea, every mile of its journey
discovered some curious or novel feature to the passengers.   Gordon sat throughout the journey, note-book
in hand, jotting down facts for future use.   Looking up
from his memoranda he said suddenly, as if there was a
missing link in his observations : " Is it not singular, Mr.
Barnett. that in a world so skilled  in the use of all

forms and developments of electricity—you said they run these air-ships by electricity?"

"Not exactly, but it is the only word we have that in any way could apply to the force exerted."

"Let us call it electricity then. Is it not curious, I was about to say, that we see no telegraph, telephone or telephote wires. That play, for instance, must have been really played somewhere. How did the Professor turn it on?"

Barnett spoke to Master Profundis for a few moments and then answered:

"It was played in the city last night, exactly as you saw it."

"Was it played for our special benefit?"

"By no means."

"Played for the whole city perhaps?"

"Played for the whole of Mars. It was an important revival, and was produced at the principal theatre in the planet. The short afterpiece was differently rendered. The original of what you saw was played at a private performance some time ago. That pretty girl so like the Professor's daughter—"

"We all thought it was Mignonette herself."

"The resemblance is very great. The girl is, or was, one of Mignonette's cousins."

"Was?"

"Yes, she has been dead these three years. The production of the play was phonographic."

"Perhaps the wires are underground," Sir George hastily suggested by way of changing the subject. The gruesome incident related by Barnett came upon them with a shock.

"All wires ought to be underground. If they have not managed that yet I shall certainly start a company," here he pulled out his pocket-ledger, " with a capital of say—"

"You are forestalled, Sir George. There are no wires!"

Sir George put up his ledger disconsolately. "No wires?"

"No. Telegraph wires are only a childish invention. Even our own great electricians already dream of dispensing with them."

"What do they use here as a substitute?"

"I only know the theory to-day. I shall understand its working to-morrow," Barnett spoke with the curious but not boastful confidence now familiar to his audience.

"Meanwhile let us have the theory," Blake suggested.

"Complementary mechanisms are constructed. These answer only to each other, but fifty or five thousand mechanisms may be constructed, all answering to one, or *vice versâ*, one to the five thousand. A message of sight or sound is flung upon the air, is plunged into the sea, is fired into the ground. At the end of its journey—be that a mile or a million—it is picked up by the waiting machine, which can only hear what its fellow may say, or see what he may show. Thus that play was probably attended simultaneously by persons distant from each other many thousand miles."

"It is marvellous," said all.

"No, it is not marvellous," Barnett exclaimed warmly; "I say it is not marvellous that a couple of machines on puny Mars should act upon each other by means of that electric or ethereal force which permeates all material things, all immaterial space. Why, this same force will transmit a solar ray at the rate of two hundred thousand miles a second, and reproduce through a spectroscope at the end of a hundred million miles the various colours of its composition, as if it had just left the sun. That is marvellous—the Martian telegraphs are children's toys."

"They are quite far enough advanced for me, at all events," Blake said modestly:

They were now passing over the outskirts of the city. For an enormous town there was a strange absence of straggling suburbs. The country ended as abruptly as the city commenced. This was because no one lived in the immediate neighbourhood of the city. It was a mere workshop—but a charming one. Time and distance were of no importance to the Martians. Master Profundis reached his destination at the central station. The air was swarming with air-ships of all sizes. Neat little yachts, comfortable, roomy ships, enormous galleons were coming and going in swarms as thick as locusts; and without beat of paddle or whirr of screw, or flap of sail!

Under the guidance of the young Martian the little band of tourists from another world started on their walk through the city. Like little children or men who had walked in darkness all the days of their life, they saw but did not understand. The City of Delight was beyond their grasp. They could not comprehend its true significance. They could only wonder vaguely at its beauty and marvel at its magnificence. They were oppressed by its grandeur. Even its simplest details were passing strange.

There were no streets—only broad boulevards lined with flowering shrubs. The shops were only vast stores. There was not a single "window" in the city. There were no screeching trains overground or underground, no lumbering 'buses, nor wrangling cabmen, nor jostling crowds, nor—best of all—no slums. But instead, there were many beautiful gardens surrounded by vast villa-like buildings and grand squares enclosing woodland groves. Grave men and beautiful women arrived momentarily from every distant mansion and moved gracefully to and fro, arranging, directing, and overseeing every kind of business in the shops, the theatres, the libraries, the picture-galleries, and other places. Directing only, for all arduous labour, all monotonous detail was discharged by that bound giant of theirs, whose tiny relative on earth we call electricity. This beneficent giant worked with

out the smoke of dismal factories, the din and dirt of
machinery, the crude device of rails, the roar of express
trains, the blundering helplessness of ponderous ships:
without the grinding misery of that human slavery necessary to a civilisation less complete, without its sub-stratal
squalor, filth, and vice.

The bound giant worked cheerfully, too, and the results
of his labour made the land more beautiful than even
Nature had shaped it, and the lives of men upon it more
blessed than prophecy had foretold. He manufactured
rich cloths and carried them by underground tubes to
customers at short distances, by air-ships to distant lands.
He arranged the weather to your liking. He lighted and
heated your house, cooked your food, and served it without a grumble or an itching palm. He whispered softly
in the ears of separated lovers, and sang in the open
squares of the city in a voice potent with the music of a
hundred tuneful instruments. He conjured up visions of
far-away lands, of absent friends, and at your bidding
dispelled them in a breath. He bound the living closer,
he brought you back your dead. He was everywhere
and did everything—a silent, but momentous witness that
the sorrowful days of human toil were passed away, that
man on Mars had mastered force.

But the knowledge of these things came slowly to
earth-clouded brains. To these wondering souls the City
of Delight was a sealed book for many a day.

# CHAPTER XV.

## THE MILLENNIUM.

NEARLY two months passed away in a peaceful, idyllic life. The party from the Earth quickly lost the capacity for being surprised. The wonders which crowded thick upon them during the first days and weeks of their sojourn benumbed their minds, and succeeding shocks passed unnoticed or unregarded.

It was fortunate that, at the outset, they had secured the patronage of so profound a student of science, art, literature, and social conditions as Dr. Profundis. Much that they had learned must otherwise have been lost. It was, indeed, a peaceful life, notwithstanding the marvellous inventions of material science by which they were surrounded—and yet not wholly satisfying. For these restless beings from the striving Earth had not attained to that perfect development of brain and nervous system which is receptive only of what is unalterably perfect and absolutely true. They were fresh from a combatant age. They were not ripe for an age of complete fruition —and dawning decay.

Very eagerly at first, but afterwards with abating interest, they entered into the highways and byeways of their new surroundings. Barnett pored daily over mighty tomes of astronomical works, the pages of which, learned as he was, he studied with the halting comprehension of a schoolboy. From them he turned away at times with a sorrowful heart, and his busy, inventive brain despaired. There was nothing left on Mars to invent.

MacGregor climbed the easy mountain slopes, and set out for long voyages in the aërial ships, vainly trying to discover some new land on Mars. From these fruitless excursions he always returned disappointed. There was no unknown land on Mars left to explore.

Together, Durand and Graves roamed through the endless public galleries for literature and art, and came back crestfallen from masterpieces before which they must ever stand abashed. Neither was there anything left to achieve in literature or art in Mars.

Sir George Sterling and Blake were the most utterly undone. The vast financial schemes of the baronet, product of many a sleepless night and ponderous pocket-book, were as naught; for these sacrilegious Martians did not even believe in the sanctity of cash—there was no longer any stock-market in Mars. And the furious philippics of Blake, with all their wealth of rhetoric, passionate invective, biting sarcasm, and potential politics —in which the crash of governments echoed to every

resonant period—were all still-born.   For party government had many centuries back been sloughed off, and for a
thousand happy years there had been no politics in Mars.

But if there was nothing left to invent, explore, or
improve in Mars, there was in it a vast field for Gordon.
Endless columns of "copy" were manufactured by him
from every passing air-ship, every pretty unfamiliar flower,
every curious animal, every sweet-voiced bird, every
sweet-faced girl, and even those benign and serious men.
The pleasant sunlight, never garish, never dull, the soft
twilight, the brilliant starlight, and those two little
lunatic moons of Mars, Deimos and Phobos, which kept
pirouetting and capering over the nightly skies, setting
now in the east, now in the west, with their perpetual
transits, eclipses, and other vagaries—all these for Gordon
meant business.

In the evenings, after the Professor and his family had
retired—they always retired early—MacGregor was wont
to assemble his followers in a comfortable room in the
wing of the mansion which had been placed at their
service.   Here they criticised their new surroundings,
and not always favourably.   Mars was "slow," most of
them thought.

"Have you noticed that there has not been a single
wet day since we came?" Blake said, at one of these
meetings.   "It is a delightful climate, but I wonder that
they do not feel the want of rain."

"There has been rain since we came," Graves answered.

"I have not seen a single drop."

"Very likely. That is because it always rains at night."

Blake looked up in surprise.

"Are you serious, Graves?"

"I am."

"Then how do you know that it only rains at night?"

"Miss Mignonette told me. I met her this morning going out very brightly dressed—it was not that grey costume, but a white, violet-bordered tunic, and she wore a short purple cloak—I asked her if she was never afraid of getting her clothes spoiled by rain. She laughed at the idea, and told me it only rained at night."

"Oh, nonsense, she was amusing herself; she is getting quite artful, that girl."

"Mr. Graves is perfectly right," Barnett put in quietly. "By means of a powerful machine for electrically disturbing the atmosphere, all the superabundant moisture in the air is precipitated during the hours of the night. That is what causes the heavy clouds which our own astronomers long ago discovered to be most common in the morning and evening skies of Mars."

"I hope, Mr. Barnett, you will bring one of these machines back with you when you are returning. It is wanted badly in some places I know."

"It is not necessary to bring a machine. Its construction is very simple," Barnett replied with a gesture of quiet superiority.

"Of course everything is simple to you," Blake grumbled.

"Blake," MacGregor said in an authoritative voice, "suppose you give us the result of your investigations into the Martian system of executive government."

"Don't know anything at all about it," Blake replied rather crossly.

"Come now, Blake," Sir George whispered, "don't let Barnett have everything his own way. You will lose your reputation as a ready speaker if you knock under so easily. Have a shy at the Government. It will remind you of 'England and home.'"

"How is a man to have a shy at the Government when there is none—I mean no party in power."

"Then have a shy at the party that should be in power."

"Can't do it. There is nothing tangible to go on. How can one deal with such a medley as Mars? They have given up horse-racing, or its prototype, and yet existence continues to be tolerable—to them. They keep dogs—I mean things like dogs—but they treat them as of secondary importance to the human inmates of the home. The weather has been abolished, and conversation has not become obsolete. Women have the same privileges as men and seem nothing the worse of it. The upper classes behave quite respectably, and seem all the better for it. The lower classes have enough to eat and drink, and decent clothes to wear, and seem to like it—unlike our own very poor in whom we revel, vicariously—in all the orthodox blessings of poverty, the elevating influence of want, the refining effects of excessive work, the chastening elements of despair, the—the——"

"Excellent, Blake! I am proud of you," MacGregor shouted stentoriously. (The walls were very thick, the door was massive.) "Go on, go on."

"Yes, yes ; go on Blake. You are more like your old self to-night than you have been since we left Alaska," several voices cried.

"Thank you," Blake answered, trying to affect indifference, but evidently flattered. Even Barnett himself had listened to him attentively. "I can't go on, however; for I tell you frankly I do not grasp the system—its origin and entity, as Mr. Barnett would say."

"What is your difficulty, Mr. Blake?" the scientist asked with interest.

"The whole scheme is my difficulty," Blake replied, with a certain self-assertion he rarely showed when Barnett spoke. But his blood was up. "They don't work on our lines, they don't work on George's lines, or Bellamy's lines, or any consistent lines at all. Those who *have* don't seem to get hold of everything. as with us. Those who *have not* don't seem to get kicked out of whatever trifle they have stuck to as promptly as with us. At the same time, they don't nationalise land—they don't nationalise anything in fact. They don't State-oversee everything, State-direct anything. On the contrary, the individual is all important, the State a tradition."

MacGregor reached over and patted the politician on the shoulder.

"You have him fairly. You have scored off Barnett at last."

The score was quickly settled.

"Do you admit, Mr. Blake, that the working of the Martian system is satisfactory?"

"In its results, decidedly. But you can hardly say the 'working of the Martian system,' seeing that everything happens at haphazard."

"At haphazard! Pardon me, the very reverse is the fact."

"Indeed. Perhaps you will explain."

Blake was now thoroughly aroused. The man of science must justify himself.

He did.

"The absolute perfection of the Martian system lies in this," Barnett said quietly. "It is neither the product of a theorist nor a law-maker."

"Then of what is it the product?"

"Of progress."

"Now, Barnett," MacGregor put in, "do not be too enigmatical. Give Blake a chance."

"What I mean," Barnett explained, " is that you may chop off the head of a tyrannical king, or hang a highwayman in chains, or shoot ten thousand savages in order to remove a barrier to racial progress. But whilst these possibly commendable enterprises may be useful in disposing of elements inimical to progress, they are not intrinsic factors in it. No walled city ever in liberty or refinement advanced one step in consequence of a gruesome surplus of bloody heads stuck up above its gates. Such hideous trophies are only incidental to the city's onward march. Never surely are they captains of it."

"How does all this apply?" Blake demanded. He felt his chance of success in the debate was growing shadowy. But he was still equal to asking a question.

"It applies especially to the formulæ of those earthly theorists, whose sublime fallacies you have failed to find reproduced in Mars."

"I don't see the connection," Blake retorted sharply.

The others listened to the discussion with the greatest interest. It was rarely any one ventured to discuss a subject with Barnett.

"Then I shall try to make it clearer. Your theorists——"

"I don't say they are my theorists."

"Our popular theorists," Barnett corrected himself, " would construct a perfect community out of constituents the majority of which are imperfect; whose imperfection, indeed, is the only basis for their own theses. They propose to break down a system designed mainly for the restraining of evil influences in order to create a system in which these influences would continue unchecked. They forget that the State on which they throw so much depends, even in their own scheme, on the will of the mass of its units. These units they would restrain, reform, refine, and enlighten by an authority delegated from themselves. In fancy, they build a splendid castle, and with a method not ill-suited to the silliness of their own hypothesis, they commence by laying the topmost stone of the highest turret. This plan has never had any success in——"

"Practical masonry," Graves suggested.

"I did not intend to say that," Barnett remarked with a smile; "but as an illustration it will serve."

"Then perhaps you will explain," Blake persisted, doggedly, "how the system—the haphazard system, as I consider it—of these Martians works so smoothly?"

"As I have said, it is the result of progress, not the cause of it—that inscrutable progress which any wise man or fool can chronicle: who is he who can explain it? By it men are brought to a knowledge of what is wise, and what gives happiness, and what is right, and then they enact beneficent laws in keeping with their newly found knowledge. But they do not ordain wisdom and happiness, and truth by statute. The Martians com-

menced with the individual—not the State. They built
their house from the foundation upwards. Their scheme
of social economy did not grow up in a night. It did not
arise from chaos at the *ipse dixit* of an essayist. It found
shape in the slow evolution of solid truth."

"It is very easy to generalise," Blake struck in.
"Suppose you descend to detail, Mr. Barnett."

"The details are easily understood when you grasp my
argument. Consider: the Martians have no coinage
indeed, but they have a system of exchange not unlike
our paper money."

"It is not to be mentioned in the same breath with
it," Sir George said, contemptuously.

"Every article of merchandise, every service of science,
every individual effort is bought and paid for at precisely
its intrinsic value. But no Martian ever works for
more——"

"They certainly don't overwork themselves."

"Or earns more than he requires. Therefore there is
no scarcity for those less gifted. Neither is there a
brain-benumbing dead level of life in which the strong
dare seek no more than the weak. There are degrees—
honourable degrees—for which all strive; strive fairly,
do not turn and rend each other for them. When these
are gained they are only prized inasmuch as they confer
the power to alleviate. The strong do not oppress the
weak. They only help them in their fraility. But this

is the privilege of the strong: it is not a right of the weak."

"Then why can't we do the same and be happy, since it is so simple?"

"To generalise, because it would not be in harmony with our environments; to particularise, because that on the Earth population has not yet, as on Mars, ceased to press on the means of subsistence."

"Blake, Blake, can't you say anything?" MacGregor ruefully exclaimed. "You made an excellent start."

"I don't feel up to much of a finish," Blake answered dolefully.

Barnett arose and took a few steps across the room. He turned before opening the door, and said by way of summing up his remarks: "The same fundamental truth underlies every development of the Martian system. In what slight Government obtains, the wise command, the unwise cheerfully obey. In morals they are sublime, The hell of human passion is calmed and still. Its office—every factor in organic or inorganic life has an office—has been fulfilled. It is not therefore surprising that their social economy should differ alike from our own practice and the theories of faddists; that it should neither be a ruthless triumph of the strongest in brain or body, a saturnalia of the rich on the one hand, nor, on the other, a paradise of the indolent, a seventh heaven for the socialist sloth."

" And the grand State panacea for all the ills that flesh is heir to is a failure ? "

" Yes."

" Has it ever really been tried here ? "

" It has. Once in the ages long gone by when men in Mars striving blindly—striving nobly—after truth, urged madly on by the resistless force of progress, had cried out of their agony for some new saviour to arise and deliver them from the body of their social death, a misbegotten monster, a State Frankenstein arose and ruled for a brief span—and passed away. He was no true saviour. He was only the contrivance of earnest but short-sighted crusaders in the cause of right—a clumsy and ill-advised contrivance. His forehead was of bright gold, but his feet were of clay—the clay of fallacy. Still his advent and his exit are interesting historical epochs in the Martian archives. I have compiled a treatise on the subject for publication on our return to the Earth."

Barnett bade his friends good night and retired.

" Where are you off to Blake ? " MacGregor called after the politician, who was also leaving the room.

" I—I—I am not very well. Good night," Blake answered and disappeared.

" Did you ever know such a man ãs Barnett, Mac-Gregor ? " Sir George said. " He has got the whole scheme at his fingers' ends. Blake made a poor show."

"A precious scheme it is too," MacGregor replied. "I am sick of it.'

It must be admitted that MacGregor's opinion was pretty generally shared by his party.

And yet if there was nothing of future novelty possible under the Martian sun, nor beneath his twin moons; if material and philosophical science had been long centuries back perfected, till every natural force had been subjugated to man's service; if knowledge had grown until by its own excess it had rent the veil from every secret in the boundless fields of hitherto untrodden truth and destroyed the possibility of its farther grasp; if literature and art by constantly mending had finally ended themselves in a grand domain of sublime achievement further than which no created man might go; if idyllic social economy had followed in the wake of individual refinement till there was nothing left to fight for on Mars, hardly anything to sigh for; if the daily round of life was as even and undisturbed as the slow-recurring seasons of the planet itself, there was much that might have recompensed these restless men of Earth for the sweet monotony of absolute perfection. There was much, could they but have read the lesson aright.

There was this: in all the world of Mars needless sorrow, suffering, and death were known no more. The gaunt spectre of loathsome disease had been laid for ever by the awakened might of physiological science, and men died rarely save in the fulness of their days, free from the blight of loved ones lost when needed most, free from the fearful tearing asunder of soul and body before nature's fiat had gone forth. The ghastly demon of ruthless war had been smitten by the fiery sword of intellectual power, and the terrible spectacle of a nation's laurels being fastened round the brow of a hero, red from the blood-drenched shambles of a human massacre, was seen only in the legends of a buried past. The sordid devil of grinding, fruitless toil, with his attendant imps, starvation, degradation, and moral death, had been bound in chains by the mighty arm of moral responsibility, and human beings were no longer on Mars treated as a little lower than the beasts of the field. Education had pierced the viscid depths of poverty and had raised from bestial ignorance the humblest sentient being into the self-respecting, self-restraining ranks of knowledge. Duty had burst the icebound barriers of the rich and bid the luxurious sensualist forth from his gross palace into loving-kindness for his species. Time and distance had been overcome by scientific discoveries till there were now no weary eyes to daily watch the lonely depths of the sounding sea, beyond whose sullen moan an answering heart beat sadly back; for in the space of a day you might bridge the Martian poles, and in the space of a second, heart gladdened heart by sight and sound from far beyond the seas.

All that is dear to men born of an age where triumph
is the only guerdon had doubtless passed away. That
triumph which in elementary life is the only safeguard,
the only guarantee of continued existence—the triumph
of the statesman, of the soldier, of the capitalist; the
triumph of the college, the playground, the workshop, or
the world; the triumph of the great over the small, of
the strongest over the weakest; the strife wherein, to put
it roughly, the biggest bully wins and the weakest goes
to the wall, be that weakest a nation, a man, or a meteor
less stupendous than that by which it must sooner or
later be absorbed, devoured; all that frenzy of merciless
victory, that wild wail of defeat dear to the heart
of combatant man, or animal, or material force, was
hushed and still. Millions of years had passed since,
like all those weird denizens of the ghastly solitudes of
space, Mars had emerged in thunders and lightnings
from the nebulous fragments scattered through a thousand
million miles of silence. Born in the travail of ten
thousand blazing hurricanes, this child of matter was
hurled forward on the whirlwind of its path, and countless æons saw it pass through all its stages from an
incandescent furnace of maddened youth to a well
ordered maturity, running its race in placid content,
century by century, unharmed, unhindered by all the
throng of ever-watchful orbs who fling their arms
through space and drag the unwary travellers of the

universe into the hungry caldrons of their never satiated appetites.

And in like manner on the sloping hills and pleasant vales of Mars, the children of its womb had grown from barbaric, merciless youth, had passed through the embittered strife of striving, starving, hungering and thirsting adolescence, and now like the orb that gave them birth they were given a brief period of bliss to enjoy the fruition of all that ceaseless travail of the ages. The stormy trials of virile strife had followed the savage griefs and brutal joys of awakening volition and made way for the contemplative happiness of an end achieved. Discordant and destroying influences had ceased from troubling, and all they that were weary on Mars had long since been given rest.

# CHAPTER XVI.

### THE PROFESSOR'S CHOICE.

MIGNONETTE made rapid progress in the language of the strangers. She did not, indeed, grasp its whole drift with the extraordinary facility of the Professor, but that could hardly be expected. Having made herself acquainted with a tolerably complete dialogue for ordinary purposes, she aspired to higher flights. With nothing less than a perfect English education would she be content. To this end, she secured the assistance of Blake and Durand. Their services were cheerfully given. The two strove valiantly to maintain their treaty. Blake rigidly refrained from the slightest effort at establishing a flirtation. Durand made no love—for a time.

During the days when Mignonette was wandering in childlike helplessness through our fearful linguistic pitfalls, Blake's ready loquacity made him the more welcome teacher. But Durand advanced steadily in the favour of the winsome maid of Mars when she began to master the useless, stupid and wearisome complication of sounds which help us to an interchange of thought. Then Blake, always of a cheerful disposition, took to instructing Mignonette's pretty little chum Daisy, whom he taught to murmur simple commonplaces seductively. Another stately girl-friend, of an artistic turn, was meanwhile posted up by Graves in the various styles of terrestrial art. And the fathers and mothers of these pretty girls did not seem to mind it. Evidently it did not occur to them that harm could come of an arrangement so innocent. Truly a strange people!

Now one day, having all attained to a fair proficiency in earthly language, these girls bethought themselves that they would like to read something of our written history, and see something of our revealed art. In other words, they asked Durand for the loan of a few books, and Graves for a private view of his portfolio. It was then that Dr. Profundis spoke. He was a grave man and courteous, but there was a moral strength about him that was rather impressive. He had heard the natural request and saw the look of indecision which passed between Durand and Graves. He drew them apart and said with great politeness and many apologies:

"Gentlemen, I heard what my daughter and her friends have requested from you, and it pains me to interfere. But I have no alternative. I have read many of the books you were kind enough to lend me, Mr. Durand, as a necessary and—pardon me—disagreeable duty—a duty which was undertaken solely in the interests of scientific research. For the same reason, Mr. Graves, I have gone through your portfolios. I am glad that the girls should take an intelligent interest in your distant Earth, and shall be pleased if you will oblige them——"

" With very great pleasure ! "

" Thank you, but "—the Professor paused, his instinctive courtesy clogged his words. He hesitated. He had almost given way when he caught the eye of Madame Profundis. She was looking at him with an air of calm, almost stern, resolution. The Martian matron was inexorable. The Professor faltered no longer. " You will please— first submit to me what you propose to lend."

" Oh certainly, sir."

Dr. Profundis hesitated again, but duty is paramount to everything on Mars—even to politeness.

" You will think me strange, I fear," he explained. " Supervision of this nature is never exercised by us—it is never necessary. I can only apologise by saying that your literature in its higher and more realistic branches—strange that you should use the word ' higher' in this connection in an opposite sense to what you usually attach to it—is too strong. Its deification of the most elementary functions of organic life is too sensual and silly. Its beatitudes of blackguardism are too repulsive and sad. Your writers of this class (Durand's books were unfortunately mostly what is called 'realistic') appear to think they have achieved an intellectual triumph if they succeed in searching out some hitherto unnoticed or undescribed human weakness or wickedness. Then as to your art—well we shall talk of that again. I weary you."

An awkward pause ensued. Durand mentally ran over his scratch collection.

" I have a book of Ruskin's about girls——"

The Professor deprecated the suggestion by a polite gesture and said : " I thank you for mentioning that author first. He is indeed high-minded, but—you will excuse me—our girls are very—very sensible."

Durand then floundered through his meagre stock, all of which the Professor had glanced over. Every title was suggested without success. The Professor, now that he had made a stand, was a scathing critic. Even the best were not good enough for him. The worst were sharply dismissed. There was too much bloodshed in Scott; too much pathos in Tennyson; too much bitterness in Thackeray; tediousness in Eliot; morbid nonsense in Hugo; balderdash in Dumas; brutality in Tolstoi; bestiality in Zola.

"Moreover," said the Professor, "there is another question besides the avoidance of what is deleterious; there is the question of what is serviceable, of what will repay the time expended in its perusal. I hold in my hand "—Dr. Profundis had learned some of Barnett's professorial tricks of expression—" I hold in my hand a copy of a work which is no doubt of profound interest to the archæological student. Its extreme antiquity renders it a literary curiosity, but it is altogether too dull for girls. I understand it is a relic found in your great Pyramid."

"No," said Graves, who was nearest to him, "it is 'Macmillan's Magazine.' "

"Oh, pardon me," the Professor hastily ejaculated as he adjusted his spectacles, "I meant no offence. I regret my stupid mistake."

One last effort of despair was made by Durand.

"I have a little thing of Browning's."

"Thank you," said the Professor, "I shall take that."

"And I," said Graves, who wished his manifold "studies"—represented as they were with all the liberty of the old Masters and all the suggestiveness of the new— at the bottom of the Maraldi sea, "I could let you have a few copies of Turner's landscapes and sea pictures."

"I shall be obliged to you for them," the Professor said with animation.

Blake did not wish to be the only non-contributor.

"I can lend you," said he, "a speech by Mr. Gladstone; I have it in pamphlet form."

"Sir," said the Professor, with the nearest approach to enthusiasm he had ever shown, "I am indeed your debtor."

The book, the pictures, and the speech were quickly brought and handed to Dr. Profundis, who received them with a gratitude too sincere to be mistaken.

"Gentlemen," he said, "we rarely or never refuse our

children anything in Mars, but I may as well admit that my daughter's thoughtless request put me in a serious difficulty. You have extricated me nobly."

He tucked the parcel under his arm. (Blake afterwards declared that he saw him wink—but that could not be.)

"A poem by Browning, a picture by Turner, and a speech by Gladstone! They are clever girls, gentlemen, though I say it myself. But if they make anything out of these I shall—I shall be indeed surprised, and you know we look on surprise as a barbaric emotion."

As the good Professor went off with his treasures he emitted a sound that might be likened to an ethereal chuckle.

Mignonette upbraided Durand privately.

"Why did you send me that silly poem when I expected one of those strange tales you often tell me" (with judicious eliminations, she might have added)?

"It was not my fault," Durand explained. "The Professor did not like our books, and—and—he thought it better for you not to read them. I will lend them to your brother."

"Very well, I always read everything my brother reads."

Durand looked anxious.

"Why not? If I don't read yours, he will tell me all about them."

"I'll take good care he doesn't," Durand said, with decision.

"You will take good care he doesn't! I fear, Mr. Durand, you are assuming an authority we are not accustomed to." Mignonette's blue eyes clouded. She was not angry—only sorry. She liked Durand, and was distressed when he did anything out of keeping with the placid ways of her world.

"I mean I shan't lend them to him," Durand hastily added, clutching at any straw in his extremity.

Mignonette rose and said coldly: "I am not yet accustomed to your manners, Mr. Durand, we only trouble each other. I will go."

"No, Mignonette! Ah, no! Stay with me, and I shall tell all about these stories—all you would care to hear. Stay with me a little while."

"Why, you curious man, how easily you become excited! We never go on like that. Of course, I shall stay. I could not bear to see you so distressed."

"Ah, Mignonette, in this world of maddening monotony, you do not know how to feel." (He was drifting fast.)

"I think you are wrong," Mignonette said, giving her pretty head a wise turn. "The only thing we do not know how to feel is misery."

"If you have never felt misery, you do not know the real joy of happiness."

"Now you are strange again," Mignonette replied, her sweet face wearing a puzzled look. "What queer things you say; one must be miserable in order to be happy. I do not understand. Do you really think so?"

"Not exactly as you express it," Durand said, smiling, "let us forget the subject."

"Yes, and you will tell me about about your Earth. You promised you would. Come, sit here, beside me." The girl placed a low chair for Durand—in Mars politeness between the sexes is reciprocal—and reclined on a richly draped couch near him.

"Now sit here, where I can see your face, and tell me—tell me one of your grand stories. I am so curious."

"It is a mercy that even that womanly trait survives in Mars," Durand thought, as he seated himself obediently.

The day was failing. That strange soft Martian twilight was stealing in upon them. Through a window of tinted glass, a ray from the setting sun pierced the mellow gloom and fell upon the face of the story-teller and lighted every flitting emotion that passed over it. What a strange face it seemed to Mignonette, as she lay back, and watched the strong light and shade in every line of it! How different from the gentle faces of the men of Mars! How hard at times and stern! How exquisitely soft when he told the rapturous story of earthly love! How pitiful when the never-ending tale of earthly sorrow must needs be dwelt upon! How fierce and fear-less when the wild magnificence of earthly combat was his theme, and his blood surged riotously through his veins! Ah, Mignonette! do not look so raptly on that face. It will bring you the only knowledge that you lack—misery.

Through an open casement came the twittering of the nestling birds. The twilight deepened, darkened—and still he spoke, and with breathless wonder and some-times awe the girl listened. Here was an orator fresh from those romantic fields of struggle long since passed into the shadowland of memory on Mars. Here was an actor, who rendered his lines with the vigour of one who had in his own person borne a musket in the fight. To Mignonette, this warrior from the fighting age was as picturesque as to us might be a Viking or a Minnesinger, could such as they step forth from their forgotten sepul-chres, and clothe their mouldering bones in flesh, and sing their songs, or vaunt their deeds in our own pre-sence. More, far more; for, like England's poet, he had the gift to tell in words of fire the drama of the heroic epoch, and the grace to select his scenes with fitting care for her whose pure heart trembled whilst he spoke.

As they sat together, the gorgeous draping of a door-way parted, and the youth to whom Mignonette was engaged, entered the room. His footfalls made no sound on the deep pile of the heavy carpets. They did not hear him enter. He stood for a moment regarding them. His face changed slowly. That all pervading expression of perfect happiness so universal in Mars passed from it. He did not interrupt them. Without a word, he went sorrowfully away.

Mignonette sighed a little melancholy sigh and murmured : " It is very grand, oh, it is very grand, but so sad, so terribly, and inexpressibly sad. We have stayed too long ; your stories interested me so much. Let me look at you again; the light is very dim. You do not look fierce now. Indeed, you are very nice." Mignonette's candour was often embarrassing. " I am sure you would not be cruel, although you are so tall and strong. I wish our men were all as tall and strong."

" They are much better as they are."

"Ah, yes," Mignonette admitted quite freely ; " I should not like them to be so dreadfully selfish, as—I am afraid—your people are—but they might be a little more interesting," she added, wistfully. " Is it not strange that I never thought them uninteresting before ? "

" Don't speak so loud, dearest. I see Mr. Blake outside there."

" Mr. Blake ! Oh, he is very kind. Why should you mind him ? "

" I—I—I don't know," Durand said, hopelessly.

" You—are—not—afraid—of Mr. Blake ? "

" Afraid ? "

"Oh, don't look so angry. I only meant what you call a joke. Don't be angry with me, please. I shall be unhappy——"

"I am not angry, indeed, I am not, but—you do not understand. Mr. Blake—likes you."

"Of course he does—and I like Mr. Blake very much!"

"Indeed!"

"Now you are angry again. I can't understand you. Why should I not like Mr. Blake?"

He did not speak. She went on simply, "I like him best of all your friends. Still, I could never like him as much as I like you. I am very, very fond of you."

"Ah, Mignonette!"

"Now you are happy again. You are so changeable. It is very interesting. I wish I could see some of your women. I am sorry your party are all men." Then with that quaint child-like truth of hers, she said : "It is a great pity. Of course, it would have been worse, if you had been all women."

# CHAPTER XVII.

## POOR MIGNONETTE.

" I HAVE something that you would like to see," Mignonette said to Durand one day, looking up at him in a pretty coaxing way, as much as to say, " Please ask me for it."

"What is it, little one?" (Durand was growing familiar.)

" Oh, something you will be pleased with. Mr. Graves did it for me. See!"' She put her hand into a pocket in the bosom of her neat little tunic and drew forth a carefully folded paper. Durand at once recognised the portrait. It was a hasty sketch of a well-known professional beauty of London.

" It is very well drawn I must say. But why should it interest me?" he asked.

" It *must* interest you," Mignonette said positively, " because it is a picture of—your sweetheart."

" Indeed! How do you know?"

" Mr. Graves told me."

" These friends of mine are altogether too friendly. Why did he tell you?"

" Because—because—I mean that I asked him to draw me a picture of your sweetheart, and he drew me this."

" Do you admire it ? "

" I don't know.   Is it a good likeness ? "

" It is a very good likeness," Durand prevaricated.

" Then I like it very much.   I will keep it.   I am glad she is not one bit nice   I should have been sorry if she was nice," Mignonette said almost spitefully.

" Why ? "

" Because you might then like her as well as——"

" As well as ? "

" As you like me," the girl said with calm candour.

" Suppose I did, you would not mind.   You have got your own—your own——"

" No indeed ! "

' What ! do you mean to say he has jilted you ?"

" Not at all.   He went away when he knew I liked you so much."

" And did not make a row—I mean he did not—did not say anything about me ? "

" Not a word.   Why should he?   He could not be angry with me for changing my mind."

" He is very obliging," Durand said.

" He is very sensible," Mignonette corrected.   " I am not yet at the age when Martian girls have to decide finally on that subject."

" Sensible !   Mignonette we shall   never   understand

each other. In our world, two or three hundred years ago, we used to fight for our sweethearts——"

"I know," Mignonette interrupted; "we have all sorts of queer specimens of the early ages in our museums."

"But we fight for them yet in some way; not perhaps with tooth and claw, or sword and gun, but still we would not give way so easily to a new-comer as that—that friend of yours. If a man acted so pusillanimously with us we would—we would dress him in petticoats. Oh, pardon me, I forgot your—your peculiarities of costume, here."

"And you would really be cruel to a man simply because a girl liked him best—perhaps you would even kill him?"

"Well, no—we are not so bad as that."

"But you would speak unkindly of him?"

"No—yes—to tell the truth, I am afraid that we would reserve that privilege—behind his back, of course."

"I don't like some of your customs," Mignonette said, in a regretful tone.

"Don't think of them, little one. It will only give you pain. Let us be happy while we may."

"Yes—while we may. I wish Mr. Graves had not drawn this sketch for me."

"I thought you asked him to do it."

"Oh yes—but—but I am sorry I asked him. I am sorry you have a sweetheart on the Earth."

"So am I," Durand reflected.

" And I wish you would not think of her any more."

They were walking in the garden. Durand stopped suddenly and stamped his foot in sore perplexity. The resolution he had made with Blake rose with a warning voice and struggled hard for honour's sake and conscience—To the winds with resolution, honour and conscience when Mignonette pleads!

" On one condition."

" What is the condition ? "

" That you will be my sweetheart, Mignonette."

" Oh yes," she said simply. " I am very glad to be your sweetheart."

" My own sweet Mignonette ! " he cried, as he caught her rapturously in his arms.

" I wonder why it is that I should like you so much better than any Martian man I ever knew ! "

" Because they do not know what love is. And I— I love you ! I love you ! "

" Ah, do not speak so wildly. It is—I think it must be —wrong to love any one so much. I wonder why it is that I feel so—so sad."

" Then I shall go away."

" Oh no, no ! That would kill me. I could not bear you to go away now. I did not mean to blame you. Only it is so strange that I should feel happy—and yet sad. You must have patience with me. You will have patience with me for a little ! "

For an answer he bent down and kissed her sweet young face, and then they walked away hand-in-hand, taking no thought of the morrow.

Only three months passed, and every man from the Earth, save two, counted the weary hours as they grew into weary days. Barnett and Durand were content. Science engaged the attention of the one, and Mignonette that of the other. Astronomy and love have always been absorbing pursuits.

All the rest were fretful. There was nothing for them to do. They were unable to take part in the working life of Mars. They found its amusements insipid. Therefore they idled, and naturally got themselves quickly into mischief—at least some of them did, and all suffered from the consequences. Sir George soon discovered that he had a mission. The terrible financial ignorance of the Martians must not continue. There was neither a court of bankruptcy nor a company promoter on the planet. Against such dense stupidity the soul of the financier rose within him. And Blake, appalled by the want of executive Government, or the want of an executive Government to denounce, was ripe for any scheme which promised excitement. Little Daisy had ceased to charm. She knew nothing about politics, and cared nothing. Gordon, overwhelmed at last by his own unfitness to grasp the Martian system of social economy, had given up his note-book in despair.

Graves had one day dropped his sketch-book purposely
into the rippling waves of the Maraldi sea. The stately
girl, whose artistic education he undertook, was wanting
in an all-important faculty—admiration. MacGregor
frankly admitted that he was bored. Barnett lived
almost wholly apart from the rest, and spent his days in
constant communion with the Professor. Durand, always
inclined towards sentimentalism, became gradually morose
and gloomy. Even sweet Mignonette, whom every one
of them worshipped after his own peculiar fashion was
not the bright angel of the vision. That strange
ethereal happiness which used to shine so radiantly from
her soft eyes faded gradually away. She became restless, then silent, then sad. Durand was often with
her—always with her.

The great interest too, which the arrival of MacGregor's
party on the planet had created quickly subsided. Nothing could have been truer than the Martian professor's
jesting allusion to the absence of surprise from amongst
the ordinary emotions of his people. For some weeks
there had been a constant round of assemblies, outdoor
and indoor, in honour of the courageous travellers. Then
the easily satisfied curiosity of the Martians wore off, and
the foreigners were of no more account than ·a new
arrival at our Zoo. It must be remembered, in justice to
the people of Mars, that the great venture of the Steel
Globe bore no such grand proportions to them as it must

for many centuries maintain to our more backward planet. The histories of Mars recorded many similar trips to the neighbouring planets. The Martian explorers, however, were always unfortunate, inasmuch as they were never successful in meeting with a world at a similar stage of development to their own. They found the Earth scantily inhabited by a few tribes of aboriginal savages. These voyages of discovery were only made in the old days of Mars, before its people had lost the attribute of physical courage—in that brief borderland of progress when nervous force shakes hands with scientific insight, and commits the future fortunes of a system of sentient life to its care.

So, in their placid happiness, the Martians grew daily less curious about their visitors. The visitors grew daily more impatient of an existence, the very essence of which they were unable to appreciate.

One day when Blake was walking in the grounds he met Mignonette. She was dressed in the same morning costume of pearl-grey which she had worn when he saw her first on the morning of her return to home. Her movements were as graceful as then, her dainty limbs were as supple, but there were dark lines under her eyes, and her soul shone through them with a new sad light—and she plucked the pretty blossoms which used to be her tenderest care, and pulled them nervously asunder, and scattered their fragrant petals on the path.

Now, Blake, as has been already admitted, was in all

respects, save one, a very estimable gentleman—perhaps even in that one weak point his polemical delinquencies were more of a necessary armour for the fight than inherent carelessness of truth. He saw that all was not well with the girl. He felt that, though fortunately blameless himself, it would have been better for her and her happiness if the Indians and half-breeds had won that brief battle in Alaska. And yet he did not altogether blame Durand.

"It was hardly Durand's fault," he reflected. "The poor silly little soul would keep him always with her, telling her stories. How could he refuse? I should have done the same myself if I had got the chance—and should have been very glad to get the chance." He turned away to avoid Mignonette. Her honest blue eyes looked one through and through. He feared to have to answer awkward questions; feared that if such were put to him he could not even answer them in official verbiage. But Mignonette saw him, and beckoned to him with a pretty air of authority which he found impossible to disobey.

The girl spoke hurriedly, feverishly, and asked many questions at random of which, it was quite evident, she cared nothing for the answer. She saw that he was ill at ease, and strove to interest him.

"Oh, Mr. Blake, I remember now I wanted to ask you about Ireland. You are an Irishman, I know."

" I am, I am proud to say," Blake answered patriotically.

" What a splendid nation yours must be," Mignonette said, still striving to gain time.

" You might say that," Blake assented cordially, and with a shade of local idiom.

" I have been reading about it in one of those newspapers you lent me. It must be a very large country."

" Well, it's not so very large," Blake answered, a little puzzled.

" Not large ! I thought it must be quite one-half the Earth."

" Oh, no—not at all. It is not as large as that," Blake felt himself forced to admit, with those honest blue eyes fixed upon him.

" But, of course, it is very important."

" It is extremely important."

" I knew I was right," Mignonette said with a pleased little flutter of pardonable pride, forgetting for the moment the main question she had at heart. " Do you know how I found out how important your country is, Mr. Blake ? "

" I am sure it was in some very clever way."

" Clever ! Oh, no, it was quite simple. I found that it occupied more of the newspaper than all the other nations of the earth put together."

" Ah—um—yes of course—why not ? "

" And yet how horribly Ireland is treated by all the other nations."

" No, no, Miss Mignonette—only by England."

" England! Surely that little country could not ill-treat your grand nation. England had only three or four little paragraphs in the newspaper."

" Ah, well, you don't understand—how could you—things are not as you think—in fact things are quite different."

This lucid explanation puzzled Mignonette a little. She tried to unravel its meaning for a moment, and, failing to make anything of it, proceeded to another subject.

" There is another thing I want to talk to you about. —I hope you don't dislike talking to me, Mr. Blake."

" I don't," Blake said simply. There was nothing to be gained with this girl by any of the little wiles he had in stock; she was so exasperatingly candid.

" I wanted to ask you—" Mignonette hesitated.

" She never used to hesitate," Blake thought, but he said nothing.

" I wanted to ask you, isn't Mr. Durand a very good man?"

" He is not at all bad," Blake promptly and loyally responded.

" Not at all bad!" Mignonette's great soft eyes opened.

"I mean," Blake said hastily, "he is a real good fellow—of course he's not—not—you know, none of us are quite up to your standard."

"But you could be if you wished."

"I am not sure that we could. I am certain we would not wish to be. Pardon me, I don't know what I am saying. I mean that it is all very well here, but our people would not stand it."

"Would not stand your being good! Oh, Mr. Blake!"

"I mean they have not got such precise ideas of right and wrong as you Martian people have."

"Is it considered very—very wrong to do what is right upon the Earth, Mr. Blake?"

"I—I—I wonder where Mr. Durand is, I want to see him particularly. I am so sorry I must say good morning. I must really find Durand—or some other fellow," Blake added the last clause *sotto voce.*

"Mr. Durand is with my father and Mr. Barnett in the entertainment hall. I can't think what they are doing. They would not let me come in." Mignonette seemed ready to cry, and Blake's confusion increased.

"Oh, some astronomical discovery! Barnett is always poking about those star maps of the Professor's."

"It cannot be that. My father always tells me everything he discovers. And I heard Mr. Durand say (I never listened in all my·life before), ' I refuse to consent, were I never to see the Earth again.'" A little sob

stopped her and then Mignonette went on again, forgetting in her trouble the earthly etiquette of title about
which she was usually most particular.  "Oh, Blake,
what can they be doing to him?"

"·I haven't an idea.  What did they say to him?"

"I could not hear their voices so well as his, for he
spoke, I thought, angrily, but they talked a long time to
him, and then I think he agreed to do what they wanted.
and—as you have always been so kind, Blake, I thought
you would not mind if I told you that I am very, very,
very unhappy."

"Mind! I would do anything in the world for you,
Miss Mignonette.  Can I do anything?  You have only
to ask me."

"I knew you were very good."  She came up to him
and put her slender white fingers in his and said very
sweetly : "Thank you, Blake.  Will you—will you ask *him*
to come to me here?  I wish to speak to him particularly."

"I will, Miss Mignonette; but—is it wise?"  Blake
said this with a certain desperation.

"Wise! certainly it is wise.  It will make me happy."

"Then I shall do it."

As Blake hurried away he muttered to himself, "This
is worse even than I expected.  I would not be in
Durand's place for a post in the next Cabinet.  That girl
is too soft-hearted and too good to be trifled with.  Little

Daisy suits me better—lots of fun and little sentiment about her!"

"What is wrong, Durand? You look ghastly," Blake said, as he almost ran against his friend who was rushing from the house, apparently under strong excitement.

"Let me pass, Blake."

"I hope, old fellow, there is nothing serious the matter."

"Heavens, man, can't you let me pass!" Durand cried wildly. Then a little more calmly, "Pardon me, Blake, I wish to be alone for a little; let me pass."

"Certainly, Durand, I only meant a kindness. You are wanted in the garden there particularly."

"Where? where?"

"There!" said Blake, pointing carefully in an opposite direction to that in which Mignonette was waiting. As he expected, Durand promptly turned his back on the locality indicated, and walked hurriedly down the path by which the lady's messenger had come.

"I said I would not be in his place for a portfolio. I would make it the premiership now," the philosophic politician reflected as he walked away. "She is bad enough, poor girl, though I hardly think she knows what is wrong with her; but he is worse, much worse. I am very sorry about this—I am indeed."

"Hallo, Blake!" MacGregor's voice called.

Blake turned down a side walk and in an open space

in a thick grove found all his comrades except Durand assembled. From their serious looks it was evident some weighty matter was under discussion. Barnett appeared to be president of the meeting. Blake was welcomed warmly. His counsels, if somewhat flippantly worded, were not regarded lightly by his friends.

"Come here," MacGregor said. "We were waiting for you."

Barnett repeated for Blake's special information a remark which he had just addressed to the company.

"Mr. Blake, you are aware that we intended to remain on Mars until the next conjunction of the Earth, which will take place in about two of our terrestrial years."

"Be the same more or less," Blake put in carelessly— the solemn faces of all annoyed him. If there was anything to discuss, let it be discussed pleasantly.

"Two years, less"—Gordon had mechanically pulled out his note-book, but recollecting in time that it was Barnett and not MacGregor who was speaking he stopped abruptly.

"Circumstances have arisen," Barnett continued, without noticing the interruptions, "which make it in every way advisable that we should start immediately. Fortunately we can still make the Earth. Had we remained another month it would have been dangerous to try it. This was what I had in view when I started from our world a month before Mars was in direct opposition. It has given us time to see a great deal and still return without the long delay of waiting for another conjunction."

"For my part," said Blake, "the sooner you start the better I shall be pleased, but perhaps I may be allowed to ask the nature of these circumstances which have happily hastened our departure."

"You have an excellent claim to that information," Barnett said coldly. "In the first place, this company which Sir George Sterling has—most unwisely, in my opinion—endeavoured to float for the object of watering the deserts of the equatorial continents of Mars has given grave displeasure to the Martian senate who do not like innovations."

Sir George looked guilty and kept silence.

"In the second place, Mr. Blake, that address which you delivered to the young men of Lagrange on the subject of Parliamentary Government, and which created so much public attention, has been no less unwelcome."

It was now Blake's turn to hang his head.

"And as for Mr. Durand——"

"Oh, I know what he has done," Blake thought.

"He has been still more unfortunate. I do not wish to speak of his indiscretion further than to say that when the unhappiness which his continued presence here must cause was pointed out to him, he acted like a true gentleman. I do not care to dwell on this matter. Let it suffice that it has been decided upon by myself and Dr. Profundis, that we start at once for the Earth—and privately."

"And besides," MacGregor added, "we are all tired of Mars. There is nothing in it—I mean there is nothing for us to do. Barnett has more packed up in his brains than will serve to advance the Earth a thousand years in science."

Blake took Barnett aside and said humbly : " I am very sorry, Mr. Barnett, if I have been instrumental in any disappointment you may feel."

" I do not blame you, Mr. Blake. You have all acted extremely well considering the whole circumstances of our journey," Barnett said very kindly.

" Then perhaps you would not mind telling me, sir— for I think I know Durand's transgression—how did you get round him ? "

" Get round him ? What do you mean ? "

" How did you prevail on him to give up—the girl ? "

" By reasoning with him."

" What reasons did you put forward ? "

" I do not care to discuss the subject further. The reasons were sufficient. Mr. Durand now sees his duty clearly, and appreciates the utter madness of his conduct," Barnett said, and turned away.

Blake left the party and walked by himself along the pleasant, tree-shaded pathways. After all, now that the time had come to leave this peaceful land of placid content, it did not seem so wearisome. Indeed, it seemed rather enjoyable than otherwise. And Daisy, too, if not so attractive as Mignonette, was in truth as sweet a maid as any man might woo.

"I would run over and see the little thing before we start, only I can't fly like these Martians. Let me see, we shall get back about the 26th. The House meets on 14th prox. I shall just be in time. What a treat it will be to smash up the Chancellor of the Exchequer over that iniquitous tax he proposes on eye-glasses. Confound these young Martians. They made a great fuss about my speech, and now it seems they have gone and told tales. Just like them ! "

The fact was that some youthful Martians, possessed of a rudimentary faculty of enthusiasm inherited from bygone generations, had made some little stir over Blake's great speech. Next morning, when they came to think it over, they decided that things were much better as they were. Excited by the orator's eloquence, they had accepted his theories of the glorious past, but they cooled down very quickly. To use Barnett's simile, they were like an old man who, heated by wine or discussion, brags about his youth, but who, when his sober moments come again,

would not, if he could, live that youth over again. He
loves to ponder over the halcyon days, sometimes—perhaps too often—he brags about them. But that is all.
He does not want them back. They came; they were
very glorious, let us admit. They have passed away for
ever; he is content.

# CHAPTER XVIII.

### GOOD-BYE TO MARS AND MIGNONETTE.

DURAND hurried through the garden in the direction he thought most likely to be undisturbed. Mignonette saw him hastening towards her, and advanced to meet him. She was the last person on Mars whom Durand wished to see, but he did not observe her until it was too late to draw back.

"You are very pale. Why do you look so wild? What were you doing with my father and Mr. Barnett?"

Durand tried to mutter some commonplace excuse, but the girl had taken his hand in both her own and was looking at him earnestly with those great honest eyes.

"I was arranging—we were arranging—that is, Mr. Barnett was arranging to return to the Earth immediately," he blundered out, looking straight ahead, and sternly resisting the little hand that tried to pull his face down towards the pained and pleading one beside him.

"Oh, is that all! I am so glad it was nothing worse."

His heart was wrung by the careless tone in which the words were spoken, but he loyally strove to feel glad that

she took the news so easily.   To judge from his face, however, one would not have thought his effort was very
successful.

"I am very glad you do not mind it more : I thought
you would have been a little sorry," he stammered.   His
voice was breaking, but he went bravely on, "I am very
glad you are not sorry."

"Do they all go with Mr. Barnett ? "

"Yes, all ! "

"Then how can you say I shall not be sorry, Mr.
Durand ?   I shall be very sorry.   I shall miss them very
much—Mr. Blake especially."

"Indeed ! "

"And I am sure you will miss him most also.   You
and he were always good friends, although you sometimes
quarrelled in that silly way.   He likes you very well, and
said something very nice about you just now."

"What did he say, Mignonette ? "

"He said you were not very bad—I think that is what
he said, but I do not remember things in your language
very well."

"I am very much obliged to him—very much."

"I knew you would, and that is why I think you will
miss him more than the others."

"I miss Blake !   How !   What do you mean ? " Durand
asked, a new alarm rising in him.

"I mean you will be sad when Mr. Blake returns to

that terrible Earth of yours. I am so very sorry for you. You will not see your friends for a long time perhaps," Mignonette said, as she stroked his hand caressingly, and pressed her face against his arm.

"Not see my friends!" The light broke in upon him. He quailed for a moment. Then he nerved himself with a hard effort, and, still avoiding the piteous blue eyes, said slowly :

"I shall see all my friends very often, Mignonette, for —*I go too.*"

He may have done many foolish things in his life— some wrong things, but never, he thought, a thing abjectly and unredeemedly mean. He felt he had passed even that barrier now. He was wrong. He had passed it long ago ; but it was only now he knew it , now, when he was trying loyally to atone his fault.

She dropped his hand and sprang back with that nimble suppleness of hers. She looked him squarely in the face. Her eyes were wild, and actual fear was in them. Her slight form trembled as the hurrying breath came fast. Her shapely limbs twitched nervously. She clasped and unclasped her hands. When she spoke, her voice was changed. It was not the silvery accents of happy Mignonette. It was the voice of a Mignonette who had learned one all-pervading lesson of the Earth. It was a voice of sorrow, and nearly of despair.

"How you frightened me !" she said slowly and painfully. "It is a joke, I feel sure. It *must* be a joke. I don't mind Mr. Blake; but, Walter, you must promise never to make a joke like that again. I—I—am afraid I shall never be able to forget it. I shall dream of it. I shall always be in terror of it."

"It is—not a joke, Mignonette." He ground his teeth together, and inwardly cursed the day he was born; but he would be a true man now. It was his only reparation.

"Oh, I know, I know. I can't express myself properly in your language, even yet. I thought a joke must be the saying of what was not true. I know you only said this for amusement, and, of course, I know it is not true."

"But this is not a joke even in that sense. *It is true.*"

"Ah, no, no, not true. I could not bear to go on that awful journey. I have not your dreadful courage. I could not do it. Oh, sweetheart! I could not do it. You like me to call you ' sweetheart,' don't you, Walter? Let us not think of this terrible subject." She nestled up close to him, and put her soft arms round his neck with a child-like trust that sent a bitterness deeper than death through his heart.

"Mignonette," he said hoarsely, "you mistake. You— *you are not to go.*"

She looked at him a moment. A lifeless stupor overwhelmed her, and with a low moan of inarticulate anguish she sank to the ground.

He raised her in his arms, and a furious storm of words of passionate love and fruitless repentance, broke from him. Her senses came slowly back. She listened to his self-upbraiding, but only half understood the whirl of fierce reproaches. Then he stooped down and kissed her lips tenderly and reverently, with a muttered "God forgive me."

At that touch her strength came back to her. She sprang from him. "You said you loved me. It was a lie. You men of the Earth are good at lying. Leave me! Go!"

Her head was thrown back proudly. She pointed to the garden pathway with a gesture of scornful dismissal, but her bosom rose and fell tumultously, and piteously belied her words.

"It was not a lie, Mignonette. It was true. It is because it is so utterly and miserably true that I am going." He did not hang his head now. He stood with a dignity that almost won her back. But her pride had been trampled on. No woman of Mars was ever deceived or despised. She had been, she told herself, deceived and despised.

"Your friends are waiting for you, I have no doubt," she said, with forced calm. "You should not keep them. What does the love of a girl signify to them—or to you?"

"It signifies this much to me"—he spoke quietly and

without bravado—"that, only for the others, I would gladly, if I had the means, explode our ship half-way back to the Earth."

"Ah no, Walter! Do not speak in that wild way. It is very wicked to say such a thing, and you always promised to be good for my sake—but perhaps you did not mean it either," she sobbed. Her short-lived anger was past. She clung to him passionately.

"You wrong me, Mignonette. When I said I loved you, I spoke as true a word as ever fell from the lips of man."

"Then in mercy you will pity me, and not leave me," she wailed.

"I pity you, and I love you, but because I love you I must go—and you must remain."

"Oh, why?"

"I must not—dare not—tell you."

"Then you do not love me as I love you—you, oh Heaven! who have taught me to love as never a girl in Mars has loved for a thousand years. Walter, I know now you were right when you said the supremest happiness and misery went hand in hand. I have been happy —wickedly happy, I am forced to think—I shall end my life in cruel sorrow. Perhaps it is a judgment on me. I—I—did not think it was any harm. Go away —I cannot bear this torture longer. God be with you. Good-bye!"

"I go, Mignonette, but with my last words I say I truly love you. Try to forget me, and be happy again. Why should our hateful intrusion into this sweet garden of yours cloud for ever your bright spirit? Think of it only as a hideous dream, and let it pass away. And yet —and yet try to forgive me for the wrong I have unintentionally done you, and for which I shall repent as long as my life shall last. Ah! Mignon, my darling, believe me the last happy hour has passed for me when I say these words, Good bye! good bye!"

He turned away and walked back by the pleasant, tree-shaded path. His face was haggard and white, and his tall and stalwart figure stooped strangely. In his ears there rang a low moan of agony, but he did not dare to stop, nor never looked back to see the poor stricken little boy-like figure that sobbed prostrate on the ground.

＊　　　＊　　　＊　　　＊　　　＊

Late on that last evening on Mars, when Blake was wandering in the charming parterres of the Professor, a small hand was laid timidly on his arm.

"Miss Mignonette, are you ill?" he said in surprise. The girl was very white. Her hand trembled nervously on his arm. She seemed to be very weak.

"Mr. Blake," she said, with a wan smile. "You are going away to-morrow. I am very sorry."

"So am I, now that the time has come," Blake replied sincerely.

" Will you do me a little favour before you go ? "

" Anything I can do you may command."

"I have never thoroughly seen this wonderful ship of yours.  Of course I have been in often with you and Mr. Durand, but there are several things I should like to have explained to me."

"Then I shall go for Barnett, he will be delighted."

" No, please, do not.  I only want to look at it.  Mr. Barnett is busy this evening.  Come with me yourself."

Blake promptly consented, and escorted Mignonette to the great black globe, which was now all ready for its stupendous voyage.  The huge fabric loomed mistily against the fast darkening sky.  It had a weird, forbidding look of gloomy strength.  Mignonette shivered and held Blake's hand as she ascended the gangway. She hardly spoke while he pointed out its interior arrangements for the comfort of its passengers.  He did not refer to the scientific mechanism of the ship. He knew little or nothing about it.  Mignonette did not appear interested in it.  But she examined carefully, and with a minuteness that puzzled Blake, the general construction of the Steel Globe.

" What is this intended for ? " she asked, pointing to the ejector.

"That," said Blake, thoughtlessly, " is an arrangement for dropping out any disorderly passenger on the voyage.

See how it works—Oh! I am sorry I showed it to you— you look very ill. Come out into the air."

He led her out hastily, and tried hard to remove the feeling of horror which his foolish words had caused.

"Thank you, Mr. Blake," she said at length. "You have been very kind."

"It was very fortunate I met you," Blake replied.

"Yes," Mignonette said gravely, "it was fortunate." With a strange meaning in her voice, she added, "I shall remember it all."

# CHAPTER XIX.

## THE STOWAWAY.

"STAND clear of each other, gentlemen. I am about to start," Barnett called from the bridge. The Steel Globe had its full complement of passengers, and all arrangements for the homeward voyage had been completed.

"I wish the thing could be managed without this capsizing," Blake remarked.

"Can't be helped," Graves replied.

"It does feel so much worse, this plunge down than if we had the sensation of flying upwards."

"Let us have a last look at Mars, Mr. Barnett," Gordon suggested.

"You will see it for the next half hour, Mr. Gordon. We shall go very slowly through the atmosphere."

"Yes, but it will be upside down," Blake urged. "Give us another minute."

The scientist held his hand. His fingers rested on the two tiny but all-powerful screws. The men below crowded to the windows. They could see the Professor watch their ship with close attention. Beside him his wife and son were standing, all equally interested. Mignonette was the only absentee.

"Durand," MacGregor shouted. "Why are you not at a window? Surely you will take a last look at this curious world."

Durand was sitting in the centre of the floor of the globe. He did not appear to hear MacGregor's powerful voice. If he did he made no sign.

"Leave him alone," Blake whispered. "He is rather —rather queer to-day. He really does not seem to be quite in his senses—that girl you know. He will come round by-and-by."

"Poor fellow," MacGregor said. "I am very sorry for him, I am afraid he will not get out of his scrape as easily as you and the baronet did out of yours. By the way, where is the girl now? It is strange she is not along with the others watching us off."

"I don't think it very strange," Blake said thoughtfully.

"Now, gentlemen," Barnett said. "Your time is up."

The men at the windows waved their last farewells to their hosts, who made answering signals. Then Barnett touched his screws, and the ship's company scrambled by the spiral path to the opposite floor of the vessel. Above their heads they could now see the Professor and his people standing, as it looked to them, head downward. Below lay a grand expanse of blue sky—an azure ocean into which they plunged.

At the request of all, Barnett went very slowly as long as objects could be distinguished on the planet they had left. Owing to the wonderful clearness of the atmosphere, mountains, oceans, and islands could be seen distinctly until the distance had become very great. Then the land of happy, restful Mars melted into an azure mist and passed away from sight.

As the atmosphere through which the Steel Globe was passing grew thinner, the sky became darker. All the beautiful blue passed away. Thick darkness took its place. The moons of Mars appeared. The stars shone out and once more, narrowed to a circle of fierce unrefracted light, the sun glared in a canopy of black.

Durand had not spoken since the voyage commenced. His obstinate silence had a gloomy effect on his friends. The three months which they had spent on Mars had passed by pleasantly if monotonously. Now that the visit was over they all felt more sorry than they could have believed to be possible. They were a very dull party for the first few hours of the voyage. There came a change.

MacGregor, who had been bustling about in his energetic way, threw himself on a couch close to where Sir George Sterling was seated. The baronet was engaged in the revision of his grand prospectus—the grandest scheme his financial enterprise had ever yet projected.

" What are you going to call the company? " Mac-Gregor asked a little breathlessly. His constant running up and down the spiral path had wearied him. " Confound it, I must be getting fat. This car is absolutely stuffy after that glorious air of Mars. Don't you find it so, Sterling? "

" Not particularly. I shall call it ' The Inter-Planetary-Communication Company, Limited.' As to capital, I think a hundred millions would do to start with. I have not yet decided, but I am inclined to hundred-pound shares —ten pounds on application, ten pounds on allotment, and the remainder—where are you off to now, MacGregor? "

" Excuse me, Sterling. I shall be back in a moment. This car is really very disagreeable. I must ask Barnett to let us have more air."

" I think you are right. I begin to notice it also. In fact I have a slight headache from it." Sir George had been previously too much absorbed in his calculations to think of anything outside them.

MacGregor went up the spiral and said to Barnett :

" Can you give us a little more air? "

" Certainly," Barnett replied. " I must apologise for having overlooked you. I was observing a star cluster."

The scientist glanced carelessly at a register and sprang to his feet with a startled look.

" MacGregor—*the air !* "

" Is very bad. Too much $CO_2$, as you would describe it."

All the men below except Durand were watching them with some anxiety. Barnett's startled exclamation had reached them. It was of a disquieting tendency.

"Come here, MacGregor," Barnett said calmly, for he noticed the anxious faces below. MacGregor stepped on the bridge.

"You see that register. It indicates our air reserve."

MacGregor stooped down and inspected the register closely. Barnett stood silent, but his face betrayed an emotion to which he had hitherto been a stranger. For the first time in his life, Henry Barnett was in physical fear.

When MacGregor looked up from the register his face too was changed. The resolute and exultant courage had died out of it.

"It seems, Barnett," he said slowly, "that we have little or no air reserve."

"We have next to none."

MacGregor did not speak one word of complaint, but for a moment a look of reproach that he could not restrain passed over his face. Barnett noticed it and said quietly: "The tanks have leaked. They must have been tampered with since last evening. They were in perfect order when I left the car. Was any one in it afterwards?"

"I do not know. We shall ask the others, though it is too late now to get any benefit by the information."

MacGregor paused and seemed to hesitate as to how he would shape a question which must be asked. Then he said bluntly, and with a dash of his own boldness come back to him: "Barnett, have we air enough to last the journey?"

Barnett again consulted a register, and made up the time necessary to reach the Earth at the rate they were travelling. When his calculation was finished he said without hesitation: "We have not."

"Then the others must be told."

"They must; it is your place to tell them, MacGregor. You are the leader."

"Yes, it is my duty—I shall do it."

When MacGregor reached the lower end of the spiral he was met by an agitated group. They had guessed the subject of the conference above. Already every one felt his breath coming fast. The secret could be no longer kept—the air was giving out!

"Were any of you in this car late last evening?" MacGregor asked, ignoring the eager volley of questions by which he had been greeted.

"I was," Blake admitted.

"What were you doing?" MacGregor asked quietly.

"I—I—was showing Miss Mignonette over the ship."

"Could she by any possibility have interfered with the air-tanks?"

" Then it is the air ! " the exclamation broke wildly from all.

" Yes, it is the air about which we are anxious," Mac-Gregor said. The veins on his forehead were already distended. His face was livid.

" I ask you, Blake, could the girl have interfered with the tanks in any way ? I do not mean the tanks themselves, for they are strongly constructed, but with any of the very delicate mechanisms attached to them for exhaling oxygen as it is required."

" I could not say," Blake answered with difficulty. His quick breathing almost stopped his voice.

" Then we need not discuss the matter further," Mac-Gregor said. " I have, however, very terrible news to break to you all."

" The air ? "

" Yes. The tanks which should be half full now, are nearly empty. The air reserve has not been consumed. It had leaked before we started. We have not oxygen enough left for the journey."

A deep breath was drawn by every man. In dead silence they waited for MacGregor to continue. They knew he had more to tell.

" It now only remains," he said, " to decide between one of two alternatives. Barnett believes that with our present number "—MacGregor had to pause for breath, the men around him gasped convulsively—" we shall all

be dead men in half an hour." Again MacGregor stopped
for breath. *" A smaller number might reach the Earth !"*

A deep moan of anguish from above caused all to raise
their eyes. There, standing on the spiral path, they
saw that which almost caused their straining hearts to
stop.

"It is the vision!" they cried.

"It is her spirit!" Durand whispered.

"It is the girl herself, and most likely she is the cause
of our misfortune," MacGregor said harshly.

It was Mignonette. She wore the flowing, filmy
material in which she had first appeared to the travellers
from the Earth. In all but costume she was sadly
changed. Her face showed traces of recent weeping,
but now her small frame shook with tearless sobs.

"Yes, it is I, unhappy that I am. I have destroyed
you. I have heard your words," she said to MacGregor.
"I am probably the cause of this terrible accident. It
was very dark last night when I came in here to hide
myself behind these great tanks, the use of which I did
not know. I stumbled and fell on one."

It was quite true. The stowaway was the innocent
cause of the accident which was likely to cost the lives of
all. Her distress was terrible to see. She wrung her
hands in misery. The eyes of every man were upon her,
and all but Durand looked wrathfully. She cowered
under that harsh condemnation. Trembling greatly, she

stole down the spiral and sought Durand. He did not look harshly on her, but he made no sign of welcome. She put her small white hand in his. He did not put it away, but he did not answer its timid pressure. Then a great change came over her sweet angel face.

"You had better kill me," she said in a hopeless, despairing voice. "I deserve death at your hands."

For one swift second there flashed through the group of dying men—from whose lips no word of cowardice had yet fallen—a terrible feeling that Mignonette had justly pronounced her own sentence : that it was right she should be the first to reduce that ghastly total, the maintenance of which intact meant death for all. There was not a man amongst them who would not have stood, revolver in hand by the gangway of a sinking ship to see the women first into the boats. There was not a heart amongst them that would have quailed had duty bid them charge an army. But this thing of horror that was before them was more than a man might dare.

Mignonette saw that wolfish look pass round and tried to bear it. But her courage failed. She staggered, and would have fallen if Durand had not supported her.

"I—I—am afraid I have not the courage for it, Walter," she murmured. "I do not fear death, but Blake explained to me last night what must be done. Oh, save me, save me ! Do not let them hurl me into that awful space without ! "

"Not should every man here lie dead!" he answered, sternly, and then with a sudden menace in his choking voice, for the men were crowding up. "Stand back—at your peril advance another step!"

It was over. The brief hysteria of physical terror snapped like a reed at this challenge from their comrade.

Blake staggered forward and said: "Forgive us, Durand; we are not fiends; it was only a passing madness."

"I believe it," Durand replied.

Then Graves spoke. Even in this dread crisis the man's characteristic brevity did not disappear. Steadying himself by the rail of the spiral, he said: "Blake is right—we'll draw lots."

"Not all of us!" Blake gasped. "You and I, Durand, were special friends of this girl. I will—this breathing is dreadful—I will draw lots with you for which of us shall take her place."

"No," MacGregor said. His voice though changed and hoarse had something still of the old authoritative ring: "I forbid it."

The great explorer had never shirked responsibility in all his life. He had now before him a duty such as seldom falls to man—and he faced it manfully.

"There shall be no drawing of lots at present. Barnett thinks that if we were even one or two less we may live till we reach the atmosphere of the Earth. Durand, you know you are the cause of this unhappy girl's presence with us. In strict justice she should be the first—the first to go. But that cannot be allowed. We are men. I am the captain of this ship. I order you to take her place."

Durand's dark face hardened. His emotional nature—capable of any sudden heroism—leaped within him.

"It is right and just, MacGregor," he shouted back. "I'll do my duty. Good-bye!"

He rushed towards the terrible door of exit—but he was too late. Mignonette was before him. She had listened to the awful sentence. For one moment of sublime agony her spirit overcame her bodily fear. With a wild wail of horror she passed out, and her slight form flashed like a meteor as it plunged into the awful, bottomless abyss of space.

Thus the number in the Steel Globe was reduced by one!

# CHAPTER XX.

## THE END.

AFTER Mignonette had vanished, Durand stood still for a moment like a man paralysed in every sense. Then he fell forward on his face and ceased to breathe. The fatal number was reduced by two—and the Steel Globe flashed on through space. But fifty thousand miles a minute was still too slow.

Sir George Sterling, being of full habit, was the first to succumb. He lay on his back, his arms extended and rigid. The muscles of accessory respiration were already in action. His breathing was stertorous. He was in the first stage of asphyxia. Gordon, Graves, and Blake were in nearly as bad a plight. MacGregor's desperate energy kept him up. How Barnett fared no man knew.

"Barnett, what speed are you going at?" MacGregor shouted hoarsely.

"Fifty thousand miles a minute."

"Go seventy-five."

"Very well, MacGreger," Barnett's voice called faintly back.

A little turn of those twin screws and twenty-five thousand miles a minute was added to their speed. But even at that rate there was another hour to pass, and every man must die in thirty minutes.

Sir George passed quickly from dyspnoic agony into convulsions. From this state he gradually fell into the fatal calm which precedes dissolution, and lay insensible. MacGregor stooped down and softly touched the sensitive cornea of the baronet's staring eyes. The explorer had taken a degree in medicine before his wandering life began. He knew the symptoms of the case before him.

" The reflex excitability has passed away," he muttered. " He will die." Again a moment of supreme responsibility for him had arrived. And again the leader rose to it.

" Charles Blake," he said to the fainting politician, "you will be least missed. Leave us—and God have mercy upon you."

In the silence that followed, Blake's staggering footsteps could be heard as he shambled weakly across to the dread exit by which poor Mignonette had passed out.

" I—have not—strength—to open—the door," Blake gasped.

" Nor I, either," Gordon choked. He had been motioned by the terrible leader to assist the generous suicide.

" God in heaven !" MacGregor's hoarse voice broke

out, " is this to be the end ?   We who might have set
the world ablaze, to be choked like rats ! "

" Engineer ! "

" I am here, MacGregor."

" What speed are you geared up to in this ship of yours?"

" One hundred thousand miles a minute."

" Then go it."

" It is almost certain death."

" Go it, I say ! "

" Very well, MacGregor."

Another turn of the screws !  The engineer holds
doggedly to his post, and every man below falls down in
stupor.   And those cruel registers move so slowly, though
in every sixty seconds of time they mark a hundred
thousand miles of space traversed !

There is little more to tell.  Only the story of Barnett's
bravery, and the wreckage of his work and life by a madman's hand, remain.   Guided by his unerring brain, the
Steel Globe kept up its fearful pace to the last possible
second ; then it slowed down and safely entered the
atmosphere of the Earth.  When the lower strata of
atmosphere was gained he had only strength to open
the tube which he had used when testing the air of
Mars.   Through this tube a stream of air rushed into
the almost exhausted globe, and before long Barnett himself and several of the band had partially recovered their
usual health.   Sir George's restoration was not so easily
accomplished.   After trying artificial respiration and

other aids, MacGregor had to resort to bleeding from the external jugular before the baronet showed symptoms of recovery. Durand, too, was eventually brought out of the deep swoon into which he had fallen.

But all this grand adventure—all that was useful in it to science, philosophy, social economy, manners, morals, or general truth was lost by the rash act of Walter Durand. The man's mind, weakened from the moment in which he had parted from Mignonette, was utterly overthrown by her tragic fate. He refused to answer any question. Once or twice, as with some faint glimmer of reason he had turned to Blake and Graves with a look of gratitude in his eyes—but the expression quickly passed away. It was no doubt reckless in the extreme to leave a man in this state unwatched; but Durand was so quiet and so undemonstrative in his aberration that he was quite forgotten in the hurry and excitement of this safe return to Earth after so much adventure. In this way only can be excused a fatuity the results of which were so momentous—so disastrous. Many a century may pass before another Henry Barnett will arise. Nature does not reproduce her masterpieces quickly. But for his untimely fate he might have hurled forward the progress of the Earth a thousand years. And yet the work of his life was destroyed and the secrets of his giant brain were wrapped in the sleep of death by the brainless act of a maniac. Alas! that it is always thus with the brilliant, god-like science begotten of organic life. The touch of a baby's finger, the falling weight of a hair, and it bites the dust before the demon wrath of inorganic force.

The Steel Globe had fallen on a flat mountain peak, not far from the coast of Guinea. The men, as soon as all were fairly restored, pitched a tent some hundred yards below the spot where their ship lay. They brought all necessary supplies down to the tent, and then prepared for a thankful rest.

"Has any one seen Durand?" Blake asked suddenly.

Some conversation ensued in which Gordon admitted that he had heard Durand mutter that he would blow the Steel Globe to pieces, but he had paid no attention to such silly talk. Barnett had arisen on the first mention of Durand's whereabouts, and, beckoning to MacGregor, he said: "Keep them all here. Account for my absence in some way. The madman may really blow the Globe to pieces. One reckless turn of those screws would make dust of it."

"We are all as mad as he to have left him there," MacGregor exclaimed.

It was in vain he appealed to Barnett not to risk his life on the chance of securing Durand in time. He almost threatened force, but Barnett was obdurate. He would bring the madman back, he promised, but he would prefer to go alone.

It was not that he really preferred to go alone—it was

the fact that he alone fully appreciated what he was risking which caused the chivalrous scientist to refuse assistance. So MacGregor returned to the tent and waited. And the end came swiftly.

An explosion that shook the very earth beneath them startled the weary occupants of the tent.

"He has done it!" they exclaimed, awestruck.

"That is the last of Durand!" Blake said, with deep emotion.

"Poor fellow! It is perhaps for the best. He would never have known a happy day," Sir George said in a feeling voice: then in a financial one he added, "the ship is a loss, but it is not a fatal one. We can build a dozen— Are you ill, MacGregor? This terrible journey has been too much even for you. Get him something quickly. He is looking death-like."

It was long before MacGregor recovered strength to speak. When he did he said in a low voice:

"You will never build another ship, Sir George."

"I trust we shall build a hundred," the baronet said cheerfully.

"Then you will build them without your engineer."

"Nonsense, MacGregor! Why should he object? Where is he now?"

"Who can tell?" He was in the Steel Globe with Durand.

www.ingramcontent.com/pod-product-compliance
Lightning Source LLC
Chambersburg PA
CBHW011352010726
47494CB00008B/2288